DEATH OF AN INFLUENCER

AF Kerr

**Book 2 in the Richard Dickson Investigations series
is now available.**

Eyes in the Shadows

*Journalist Richard Dickson's mental state is spiralling downwards.
His desire to get out of his head and into a story leads him to Dr
Charles Mee – a respected therapist with a wretched private life.
The therapist, thrown out of his marital home, enlists Richard's
help to identify a stalker whose threats are becoming more sinister
by the day. When the stalker begins to close in, Richard Dickson
can save a life – he just isn't sure there are any worth saving.*

For Joy.

CONTENTS

DAY 1

1

Cancelled. You and me both, Richard thought, glancing at the broken-down train as he left the platform. The glass clinking in his bag drew looks from people around that were suited and booted for work. It was 8:30 AM after all. He should've followed through with the plan to fill empty water bottles, but he had talked himself out of it thinking of what he would be met with at his destination – Laurent-Perrier and Grey Goose.

Glasgow's Central Station wasn't as busy as it used to be at this time – a mix of earlier start times and home working. All that served to do was highlight the issues, both physical and societal, in its orbit. A homeless man outside the newsagents was snoozing peacefully, comfortable in the fact that most people were obeying the rules of the bubble around him and not getting within two metres. Richard considered, as he always did, buying a coffee and giving it to him. Something stopped him, again as it always did. He left the station planning to get one for himself. Over the years he had watched the city transform around him and enjoyed its current state of limbo – a clash of old and new. People asking for change collected it in recycled plastic cups from hipster cafes, and groups of silent, troubled old men propped up bars that were decorated with bicycle wheels and half a top hat. The bookies and pubs remained but were now framed by vintage clothing shops and marketing agencies. Dual fears of being either stabbed or stuck in a charity flash mob dance party were in the back of everyone's mind. Richard couldn't decide which would be worse. Eager to avoid both, along with any interaction at all, he pulled his cap down close to his eyes and walked along Argyle Street as the sun began to shine.

Sipping his drink carefully, the queue around him waiting for takeaways bulged and swayed as one. An occasional knock on his table kept him from catching up on the sleep he had cut short earlier. Red-faced office workers puffed, panted and checked the time. It made you wonder if the morning caffeine run before arriving at the office was really worth it. Maybe people were just born to be stressed. Richard could relate. He checked his emails and found nothing from the one person he wanted to speak to but plenty from the people he didn't. It was one month to the day that he had published his article online after six months of research and investigation. The praise had lasted three weeks before an abrupt U-turn, which wasn't a deal he would've taken with hindsight. He felt like a footballer who had trained for years for a top-level start only to break his leg in the second minute. The only difference was people would feel sorry for the footballer, not call him a wanker on Twitter. Yes, the social media attacks had been particularly brutal from all angles. If he was being honest with himself, it was hard for Richard to argue that he didn't deserve it. It was this that was perhaps causing the hesitation every time he found himself with his thumb hovering over the option to deactivate his account – he was taking his punishment. Still, going under the radar was preferable, which is why this weekend trip was so appealing. There would be a lot of eyes on it for sure, but he would be a disposable extra to the main feature: Ava.

At 35, Richard thought his days of receiving birthday party invitations were long gone. This was the source of his surprise as he held the elegant envelope that had arrived two weeks prior, but it was quickly outweighed by the fact it was from Ava. She was, on official records, the girl he had lost his virginity to in high school. Only he knew that the awkward fumble they had really didn't count, and he wouldn't experience that particular sensation until a few years later with somebody else. It spoke to the power Ava wielded that she was the one he remembered most out of the two. They grew apart as teenage lovers do but would still call each other friends, despite not speaking for at least 10 years. Not that it was hard for him to keep up to date with one of the most successful young women in the country. Her fame began at the tender age of 17 when TV execs visited their school. She was chosen as the face of a new wave of children's programming and remained there for a season. Curiously, she gave it all up and went into exile for mental health reasons. At this time, Richard hadn't reached out – a source of lasting disappointment and angst between them. With hindsight, the time off – during which Ava only featured in the papers sporadically via her PR team – had turned out to be a marketing master stroke. Demand for her presence only grew, and the intrigue around her disappearance made her the biggest star to not be actively working, not including the dead. When she returned at the tender age of 20, as most knew she would, her profile skyrocketed. She was, in his mind, the original influencer.

Now, 15 years later, she hadn't put a foot wrong. Richard often wondered if the fame had changed the compassionate and modest girl he was once so close with. The fact that he was about to attend her 35th birthday party on a Scottish island she had exclusively rented out told him that yes, it probably had a bit. What was to be expected of someone with cross-generational appeal like she had? She was the rare breed of celebrity that your mum would approve of and your niece would still think was cool. Richard would argue against, albeit lazily, the people who accused stars like Ava of doing nothing or having no talent. Their talent was just that – they didn't need anything else other than the skills and drive to be in the spotlight. Of course, fame brings with it more opportunity. If Ava's deals, endorsements and product lines were to be counted they would surpass the age she was about to celebrate.

Now back in the station, Richard had a look at the newsstands. The industry – his industry - was on its knees right enough. It had nobody else to blame but itself. Sure, people could get the news online, but in the face of trouble the newspapers didn't stand and fight for what they had been built upon, they stooped low and tried to sneak their way under the barrier. Instead of going digital with respectable journalism, what they had created when the time came to it was advert-plagued websites where users had to answer product questionnaires to ultimately arrive at something that was riddled with spelling errors, assumed information, unattributed quotes and auto-playing videos with yet more ads. Maybe it could be excused if the stories were worth it, but they rarely were. Tales of rehab and pregnancies, affairs and past utterances that hadn't stood the test of time. On the other end of the scale, the papers that took to their high horse were so up in the air that they were getting vertigo. In their attempts to prove they were nothing like the tabloids, they had left the casual reader in the cold with a heavy rain of ridiculous old English and pompous opinions. The middle ground? A gulf. A nothingness. A black hole that would slowly consume both poles.

To try and combat the growing pressure each outlet put on their writers to stick with their narrative, Richard had taken the decision to go freelance, keeping as best a relationship as he could with the left and the right, as well as the ones who hated or feared everyone and everything. Secretly, he preferred those ones. He had written for a lot of online platforms that were making names for themselves as real journalism, and the invoices were starting to meet in the middle. He didn't care about or chase riches because he simply knew that even if he did, they would never come. He bought a paper that had always been kind to him, one that had a good editor who pursued the truth and invested in his writers. Still, his £1 was a drop in an otherwise calm ocean.

So where were the general public going to find out what was happening in their world, if not this locally owned newsagents? Social media, which brought with it its own problems for society. An unregulated, anonymous mess where opinions travelled ten times faster than facts and were believed just as quickly. Generations had microphones and stages that could reach the world, all wrapped up in systems that were much fairer on the bad people than the good. It was demeaning for a journalist to be believed in equal measure as someone's Aunt's friend's son's barber. And yet, because of the grip of the world that social media had, a righteous stand on the matter would go completely unnoticed – for anyone to know about a boycott it had to happen on the platform, and that wasn't a boycott at all. A necessary evil summed it up nicely. He had been subject to abuse online before, mostly from people with cartoons for pictures. This particular time was different, and even worse for it. The people were real, as was their outrage.

Now on the rescheduled train, Richard's tension eased as it began to move. He was surrounded by three empty seats. A small victory that most in the world could appreciate. It was a last introverted hurrah for him. For the weekend to come he would have to be engaging, forthcoming, exuberant even. The guest list wasn't available, but one could take a guess at the type of people who would be there. Some famous, some eager to be, but each and every one of them as entitled as the next. He lifted the lid of his laptop as a stag party took the seats across from him and spilled into his personal space.

"Hold on." One of them said as Richard begged some sort of higher power that they weren't about to speak to him. "You're that journalist."

No luck. He looked up and saw what he was dealing with. Six guys with twelve open cans of beer between them. It was clear by the intrigued looks from five that only one recognised Richard.

"Yes, I am the person you think I am." He said, not really seeing much of a point of trying to avoid what was coming. It had happened before and it would happen again.

"You know what, yeah?" A London accent. "You're the fucking problem with society these days." A fleck of the guy's spit hit Richard just below his eye. It was hard to tell sitting down, but his opponent was probably 6 foot tall and 3 foot wide. If he was standing on the tracks, Richard wouldn't like the train's chances.

"Listen, I don't want any trouble. Everything I wrote was confirmed at the time. It's just that some things have –"

"It's just that you were talking shit and trying to ruin a man's life." The big man cut him off, redness rising in his cheeks. There was a lazy attempt from the rest of the group to calm him down, but it was quite obvious that allowing his anger would make for a much more entertaining journey.

"Danny…" One of them muttered, seeing Richard's discomfort.

"Mike, you know I fucking lost the gig in HQ because of what that bird said I said. People like him are the reason." He jabbed a finger into Richard's chest.

"Who the fuck is he?" Another asked.

"*He* is the cunt who wrote the story about Gary Young. Accused him of raping a bird. Turns out it was all bullshit. Almost ruined a man's life."

Now that Danny had won the emotions of the rest of the group, Richard decided it was his time to leave. He folded his laptop shut slowly and stood up. Luckily, his bag was further up the carriage. Unsurprisingly, not one of the group moved to accommodate his exit. Determined to remain calm and appear unphased, Richard took his bag down slowly and started to walk away.

"Oi." Danny shouted. Richard turned, expecting a middle finger. Instead, a full can of beer connected with his eye socket and toppled him to the floor. Saving face no longer an option, he scurried down the aisle as fast as he could, dragging his bag with him as the liquid soaked into his clothes and the pain spread around his face.

2

He splashed cold water on his face because he had seen it done in films. It hurt and didn't help at all. What were the chances of him being able to wait out the rest of the journey in this tiny, stinking toilet? Slim. At the rate Danny and his pals were consuming their beer they would definitely need to make use of the facilities. Was this what to expect for the rest of his life? Did he ever consider that the people he wrote about had this fear and anxiety that he now felt? A knock at the door allowed him to avoid answering those questions in his head. He took a last look in the mirror – it was not a cool wound. The swelling was quickly turning purple and had reached his nose on the left side. This wouldn't bode well for the superficial festivities on the other end of the journey.

The only way to go was further away from the carriage he had initially sat in, so that's what he did. A blonde woman in front of him ended a phone call and stared at him. Just as Richard was resigning himself to another berating, albeit probably just verbally this time, the look on her face turned to worry.

"Oh my God. Are you okay?" The accent was LA, and with that Richard had guessed her destination.

"You should see the other guy." Richard said. "Seriously, if you do, can you tell me what he looks like? I can't see a thing." He gestured towards his eye and the woman laughed nervously. Despite claiming he hated cliches, he found it hard to not fall into their trap often. She was wearing an oversized beige hoodie and huge hooped earrings. Her blonde hair was in what seemed like an infinitely long ponytail. She ran her fingers through it and draped it over her shoulder.

"Seriously, can I help?" She asked. A flicker in her eye gave away the hope that he would say no.

"Honestly, I'm fine. Listen, sorry if this is forward, but you don't happen to be going to Ava's party do you?" He asked, straining his good eye and feeling the battered one close evermore.

"How did you know?" She perched on the armrest of a seat beside her now. Aside from a couple of business types, they were the only two in the carriage.

"Call it an educated guess." Richard replied, but quickly realized that it sounded creepy and not cool. "You don't hear many accents like that on a 10AM Glasgow train."

She conceded with a smile. "So you're going too?"

"I am, yeah. Although I'm not sure they'll let me in like this." Richard put his bag down on a seat and made to sit.

"Oh no, come and sit with us. We're through here." He accepted with a nod, quietly delighted that he was going to first class and likely wouldn't see Danny again in his life. "And trust me – some of Ava's friends look much worse than you do." LA's ponytail brushed his chest as she spun and led him through the doors.

At the table sat two other beautiful women. In fact, it reminded Richard loosely of a dream he'd have as a teenager. Loosely in that there were three girls and him and then the comparisons ended. Almost as if planned, there was the blonde he had already spoken to, a brunette and his final travelling companion had hair the colour of fire, dyed of course, in a clear attempt to stand out in any crowd. Scotland, home of the gingers, probably left her feeling disappointed. Richard couldn't resist a smile picturing a grandmother from one of the various council schemes nodding at her in solidarity as she got off the plane. He didn't feel bad for this, because she wasn't hiding her disgust at the state of him.

"Guess what, ladies?" His handler said to her friends.

"You're being charitable?" Fire head said, blowing something from her nails. It stung more than the beer can had.

"Don't mind her. Being a bitch is kind of her thing." Added the brunette, who cemented her place as Richard's second favourite.

"This guy is coming to Ava's. Sit down." He did. "I'm Chrissy, this is Sasha and the rude one is Emily." They all waited for him to explain himself, so he did.

"I'm Richard, I'm an old friend of Ava's and someone just hit me with a beer can about ten minutes ago."

As the train passed the banks of Loch Lomond, he felt safe enough with the three of them to tell them the details, partly because the story that had started it all hadn't garnered world-wide attention. He explained that his semi-success as a freelance writer had led to a woman, Jane, contacting him with allegations of inappropriate behaviour and sexual assault against a politician. Sasha raised her eyebrows at the mention of Counsellor. In the end, Richard settled for describing him as a Mayor, which wasn't true but she got the point. After months of research and the participation of other women, all of whom made much flimsier allegations of sleazy encounters, Richard published the story on his blog. The Counsellor, Gareth Young, had ignored his attempts for comment, not believing it was any-thing to worry about unless it was coming from a tabloid. He was wrong. Overnight there were calls for him to resign and he found himself in the eye of a scandal. Richard fielded offers of interviews on daytime TV and evening news, all of which he accepted eventually. It was increasingly looking bad for Young, who denied any wrongdoing from the start and kept relatively quiet. That was until he organised a press conference and in it read a statement from the police. Jane had collapsed under ques-tioning, admitting it was a personal vendetta and that the story had been blown out of proportion. Gareth Young, in no uncer-tain terms, announced that he was suing the scum who wrote the article and coerced Jane into lying. Richard, in other words.

"So you're fucked?" Emily asked.

"I'm fucked." He confirmed.

"And the girl?" Chrissy managed to avoid saying 'oh my god' for the first time.

"She's not answering my calls. I don't want to push it, considering I'm the one being accused of harassing her now. All I know is that I wrote what she told me. I didn't change a word." The three women nodded, but whether they were sincere or not Richard couldn't tell. Again, something he just had to get used to. Maybe they were cursing the fact that they let him sit at their table. He'd put some distance between them when they arrived on the island as a thank you.

"Now that's out the way, anyone want a drink?" Richard took a bottle of whisky from his bag. He had been prying his mind from the thought of it all morning, but could fight no longer. Another cliché he found himself partaking in. They accepted a plastic glass each.

As the alcohol burned his throat and eased his face pain, Richard tried desperately to hold onto the information the three Americans were firing at him. Chrissy, who came to his rescue, was an influencer who shot to fame with home styling tips. Sasha was a make-up guru who had recently penned a deal to launch her own product line. Richard guessed that it was what she was sporting on her eyes, which were mesmerizing. Emily, the rude ginger, was on a B channel reality show. Each one of them was a bit insulted that he knew none of this already, but he did get the feeling they were beginning to enjoy his company as a sort of beer-soaked, Scottish mascot. He described the areas the train passed through to the best of his knowledge as they took pictures and posted to social media. Chrissy posed beside some of the 'young team' graffiti on one of the train seats. They sporadically broke into conversations about news from their phones, always about people Richard didn't know from places he'd never been in situations he didn't care about. When they directed the conversation back to him, it was mostly patronising.

"We just thought we'd slum it, you know? Get the real Scotch experience. We could've just flown direct." Emily told him, after calling the overweight and overworked train conductor cute. Richard accepted her phone to take a picture of the three of them. The camera was switched to selfie mode, and he briefly took in the extent of his injuries. After that, he looked at his good side and analysed himself, as one does when in the presence of such perfection. His closely cropped hair was a time saver rather than a fashionable choice. The lines around his eyes and on his forehead seemed to duplicate each time he looked. The beard he had sported since puberty allowed him was still relatively flat and unimpressive. He had never really cared about his appearance until his face had been plastered all over the internet. For the first time he had no choice but to look at himself.

As the train plowed on, his phone vibrated: a message from Ava – the first in as long as he could remember. "You're still coming aren't you? There's something I need to talk to you about."

"So have you ever actually met Ava?" Richard asked the women. They looked at one another with perfect coordination to decide who would answer. Probably the type of people to change entirely when found on their own.

"Oh yeah – a bunch of times." Chrissy answered. "We mix in the same circles. She's not *huge* in the states, but she's still known in the circuit."

Richard knew that Chrissy was making herself feel good. Ava was worldwide.

"I've hung out with her." Said Sasha. "Nice girl, but she's getting older."

"She is?" Richard asked, because that also meant that he was too.

"Well, you know – it's a young girl's game." Emily giggled but stopped when nobody joined in, and presumably when she realised she had said nothing amusing.

"You think she's on the way out?"

"Oh, I'd never say that." The three of them physically retreated as far as their seats would allow them. Richard hadn't much rated their conversation so far, but they were savvy enough to know not to gossip to the wrong people. "You said you went to school with her?" Chrissy flipped the questioning.

"Yeah, twenty years ago. It's strange to see her now."

"How so?"

"I don't know – I guess it wasn't as easy to get famous back then. No social media and so on. To think your girlfriend was -"

"*What!?*" Even before Emily's exclamation, he knew he shouldn't have said what he did. "*You* dated Ava Hart?" He didn't necessarily enjoy the intonation on the word 'you' but found it hard to disagree with.

"A long time ago. It was a teenage thing."

"I told you." Sasha whispered to the others.

"Told them what?" Richard asked.

"I was saying that sexy and handsome were out – awkward and funny are in. No offence."

"None taken." He lied. The three of them were analysing him like some spit under a microscope now and making no attempt to hide it.

"You're pretty much the only guy of hers I've heard about."

"No, stupid." Emily interrupted Sasha. "The manager."

"Oh yeah." Sasha conceded.

"Ava's dating her manager?" Richard asked, only sounding jealous because he was trying so hard not to. Chrissy glanced at her two friends, apparently disappointed at their loose lips in front of a journalist.

"People talk, but you can never be sure." She said diplomatically.

Richard took their shared looks and silence as an opportunity to look out at the landscape. The train was skirting the coast – sharp greens splitting into deep blues. He could see the attraction of coming back here for a celebration, even if the bright lights of London and, less so, LA, had drawn Ava in like a moth. He was interested not in the people she had met along the way, but how they had changed her. As the ladies started talking again, Richard looked down to his phone, angling the screen to make sure he was the only one with sight of its contents. *Who is Ava Hart's manager?* He asked the search engine.

3

Ava Hart was an enigma. It seemed that she delighted in doing the unexpected, changing directions the minute she was in danger of being boxed into a category. Despite that, the one constant in her career was success.

"Where do you want the bar, Miss Hart?" As she pointed the man in the right direction, she wondered who had made him address her like that.

"Call me Ava." She shouted after him. He didn't acknowledge it.

Was this a bit much? Of course it was. There were 30 people around her working on preparing the weekend's festivities. Soon they would be shipped off the island leaving only Ava, her staff and her 200 or so guests. She was going for a festival vibe, much to the unuttered annoyance of most of the invitees who would be swapping their usual five-star hotel rooms for tents on the deserted island. Still, she knew some of them would bend the rules and have elaborate camping equipment flown in. She could hardly complain, as she had the only house.

The sun warmed her thoroughly as she looked out past the cliff edge and into the water. She felt calm with a slight hint of tension brewing. The island was exactly what she pictured – Tara, her assistant, had done exactly what was asked of her for the thousandth time. The green landscape twisted and turned, rose and fell at sharp angles. Small inlets of water separated a few segments of land that looked as if they were trying to break free. Any of them that made it far enough had been engulfed by the ocean. Maybe, Ava thought, that was to be the fate of the whole island. She had been keynote speaker at a climate change conference a few years prior, and rising sea levels were included in the notes she read on the private jet they sent to pick her up.

The house behind her had clearly been kept well over the years. It had the lingering smell of firewood that you expected from the countryside, and solid walls designed to protect any guests from the strong winds on the island. The rooms were all rustic and practical with large windows at every possible turn complete with stunning views. She had noted earlier that the balcony accessed from the master bedroom was a perfect place to look out on the party later – it didn't bother her that most people would take this as a show of superiority. She had rented an island, and when she paid the tens of thousands of pounds for it she also handed over any opportunity to appear modest. On more than one occasion, Tara had tried to find out her motivation for this particular extravagance. "It's just not you." She had said, followed by "I mean I know you hate half of the people who'll be there." She wasn't wrong, but more would become clear to her soon. Ava had created a perfect image of a powerful woman – one who was in control of her own future. She desperately didn't want to be a fraud, but the truth was that she had been at the disposal of powerful industry people since her first day on screen. More in control than others she knew? Yes, but that wasn't a victory in her mind. This weekend, and the rest of her life, was to be different. Although she was forever accompanied by Tara, and she had given her life to her career in more ways than one, she had loneliness and sadness within her that she couldn't shake. Now, on the eve of her 35th birthday, she was ready to do the unexpected one last time. Plus, she had wrongs to right and she was beginning to feel as powerful as the image they had given her.

4

"Don't do that." The captain said. At least, Richard assumed that's what he should be called. It being a speed boat didn't matter – he was driving so he was the captain. Richard brought his hand out of the water like he was told and muttered an apology.

"Is it your island?" He shouted to be heard over the engine. It was met with a hearty laugh.

"No, son. I just manage it. Owning an island wasn't in the stars for me." He leant his head forward and concentrated on the water in front of them. Conversation over then.

Richard guarded his eyes from the sun to get a better look at their destination. It was as authentic as it gets. He hadn't had the headspace to do any research into it before coming, so to him it was called Ava Island as per the invitation. As they progressed, it was like he was entering a screen saver – small beaches, vibrant blues and greens, cliff edges and what looked like a lighthouse. The sun soothed the pain in his eye as he searched the surrounding area. Nothing but ocean. He stopped his hand reaching for the water again. He thought of leaning to the side enough so that he would fall in, skipping like a stone once and then submerging and dropping as deep as he could. It wasn't the first time such thoughts had crossed his mind. He didn't think he was suicidal, but he knew that disappearing would be easier than the next few years of his life. That didn't seem like depression to him – in a way, it was positive thinking. He often told himself he had nothing left, so why stick around? How could he possibly begin to write his next story? This place should be utopia for a writer, even one whose focus was the rich and famous. He started out finding the inspiration to investigate in the simplest of things, but nothing came to him now. The man of five years ago would be fizzing with excitement at the potential insights he would gain from such a group in such a place, but the crisis of confidence he was experiencing had left him struggling to write a birthday card. He looked at the waves again and slouched deeper on the narrow seat.

The American girls had organised a ride with someone they knew at the harbour. It was a yacht that had plenty of room for him too, but he didn't push his luck and said he would catch them later. Besides, he was getting a bit tired of the conversation. They were dropping names like their country dropped bombs. Plentifully. So, arriving alone it was. Finally, he could see activity on the shore. Judging by the amount of people already there, he wouldn't be shocked if he didn't cross paths with Ava for the entire weekend. It wasn't only her peers that would be there – it would be her contributors. A few years back, she had shunned the major TV networks and even the big online platforms. She created her own channel against the good advice that people wanted more than just her content. To remedy that, she brought on other personalities and offered exactly that. It was the making of a mogul. Currently, she hosted a chat show and took people behind the scenes of her life for an hour per day. Everyone wanted to be a part of what she was doing, whether they liked her or not. Incidentally, Richard got the feeling that his new friends from the US didn't like her. They were essentially here to make themselves known – an interview of sorts. If he knew Ava as he thought he did, she would know this fine well.

He was off the boat on rocky sand as his prediction was proved incorrect.

"Dick Dickson. Do people still call you that?" Ava Hart was stunning. If her features were described - the sunken eyes and the small, slightly curved nose - they could be interpreted as flaws. They weren't.

"You're half right." He smiled as she approached and they fell into a hug. Old habits. She moved him away and kept her hands on his shoulders to examine his eye.

"Jesus…" Ava had already correctly assumed what led to it.

"You're getting it rough aren't you?" They began a laboured walk on the uneven surface. She handled it much better than he did.

"Don't worry about me. Anyway this is Ava Island, not Dick Island."

"You might think differently when I introduce you to some people."

They laughed together and then felt silent. Richard wasn't planning on asking her to explain the message she sent to him, so it hung in the air between them and would continue to do so until she saw fit. He stole quick glances at her as she hiked up a hill in front of him. The champagne lifestyle hadn't hurt her figure, which was hugged tight by fitness gear. Her platinum hair – the latest of many colours – shimmered like the ocean he had crossed to see her. Not that they would ever be more than friends again. Actually, even friends would be a stretch just now. How different would life be if they had stuck with their daft, childish relationship as so many others do?

"Are you looking at my arse?" Ava said, reverting seamlessly back to her Glaswegian accent.

"It's right in my eye line."

"That ship's sailed. In fact, it set sail, the crew got plastered and it sank after hitting an iceberg head on." She didn't look back, but he could tell there was a smile forming.

"Island patter. Good stuff."

"Plenty more where that came from, Bucko."

"You should've said booty, you know." Richard said. Ava giggled and waited for him to reach the flat land at the top. When he was level with her, he couldn't hold out any longer.

"Listen, you'll understand if I'm a bit confused by all of this."

"You mean why did I invite you? You're my friend." She held his stare.

"And the message earlier today?" As he motioned with his phone, he noticed the extremely low signal.

"Get settled in. I'll fill you in later. Promise." And with that, he began following her once more, just like the old days.

The camping arrangement had been a great ice breaker. Small groups congregated around the island house's garden, laughing and clinking glasses over their half-erected tents. A repetitive beat boomed from two huge speakers that had been installed that morning – a jarring sight of technology in otherwise untouched nature. There were certain privileges that Ava knew couldn't be sacrificed. Four toilet cabins, each with immaculate cubicles and showers, had been arranged. There were almost as many bars as people, and staff circled the area with trays of various drinks. A row of 50 quad bikes stretched past the house's back wall. This was all framed by the most incredible views Richard had ever witnessed. He got his bearings by focusing on one thing in each direction – an old castle to the north, lighthouse to the south, beach to the east and cliffs to the west just beyond the campsite. He dropped his bag from his shoulder and accepted a cold bottle of beer from a waiter.

"Dickson?" There were two types of people that called him by his surname – his old schoolteachers and journalists. Richard assumed the latter and was proved right as he spun round. Tabloid journalists were the one section of society that he knew he could expect solidarity from, whether he wanted it or not. Paul De Rossi was one who wore the tag of hack proudly, unlike Richard. His shirt was open by one button too many and hung over a gut that had been slowly growing since Richard had met him. His jet-black hair was greasy because he was constantly running his fingertips through it.

"Tough break on the Young story." He continued, tapping his beer off of the one in Richard's hand.

"Yeah, not ideal." He replied with the understatement of the year.

"Between you and me – did you do a bit of interpretation?"

"Fuck off, Paul. Some of us have never done that."

"Come off it, man. You were spinning more webs than Peter Parker."

Richard shot him a look that said he really didn't have anything to gain from being polite just now. That, paired with his bulging eye, told De Rossi all he needed to know. He raised his hands in an apology. They both knew that him not uttering the words was calculated. He was probably forming the beginnings of a story in his head.

"What you reckon to all this?" Paul pointed the neck of his beer in the direction of the crowd. Richard knew all too well that every sentence spoken to him this weekend would be turned into a quote for stories churned out over the next week or two.

"Must get harder and harder to spend the cash. Fair play to her." He replied.

Paul nodded, accepting that there were others around willing to offer controversial opinions as the drinks flowed.

"What about you?"

"Not like her. And I would know."

"I notice she's your bread and butter – how did you swing that?"

"I've been there from the start, Dickson. Right after you left the picture, There I was. Funny how things work out, isn't it?"

"Hilarious." Richard replied. They said their goodbyes, and with that he had got rid of his only potential companion for the days ahead.

A DJ, whose name escaped Richard, took to a small podium and began a mic check. It allowed Richard to identify the young from the old, as everyone in their twenties got ready to dance. As the crowds separated, those in their thirties were left on the fringe, smiling and maybe allowing a slight head bop here and there. They were dressed more conservatively than their younger counterparts, and smoked cigarettes rather than the modern electric equivalent.

Richard scanned the crowd and met a set of eyes that were focused on him. A sly smile spread across the face of his observer; a wine glass raised in salute. The man was Robert 'Bobby' Taggart. He had extreme family wealth, so much so that these sorts of engagements were all he had to do in life. More importantly to Richard, he was a close friend and donor to recently disgraced and then absolved Councilor, Gareth Young.

5

No matter where you fell on the political spectrum, you had respect for Gareth Young. He seemed to be an incredibly skilled politician at the same time as pointing out the hypocritical flaws within the system. Gareth Young could capture a student's vote just as he could capture your Granny's. He didn't apologise for minor laws broken or recreational drugs used in his past. In fact, he was so sure of himself that one could assume he had never conceded anything at all. As a true independent, the voting public looked to him to provide some clarity between sparring parties on the left and right. His verdict, always announced with aggressive vigour, was taken as gospel. He was more a more successful commentator than politician, but that would change quickly when his time came. Amongst his supporters was Richard Dickson. So much so, that it had pained him to hear the allegations on a wet and grey day in November. Jane - no last name given at this point and a strong hint that the first was an alias - sat across from him in a small West End café. Richard had chosen it because he knew they had one table, two seats and a staff member who busied himself in the back.

"Were you the right person to come to?" She had asked, yet to make eye contact. Her sleeves were tugged down to her fingers and she held her coffee tight as if it might escape.

"That depends on what you expect to get out of this." He replied, immediately knowing that it was a crude way of putting it.

"You think I want money?"

"No. Sorry. I didn't mean it like that. I meant... I can tell your story, but I can't guarantee what happens after." Just like that, he had committed himself to the duty of helping Jane be heard. A flash of regret stabbed his insides.

"I already know he won't go to jail. You don't know how powerful he is. Important people want him to *go places.*" Her eyes met his for the first time, telling him that it was neither an exaggeration nor a cliché.

"Can you take me through what happened?" Richard left his notepad face down on the table, hoping to make her feel more at ease. He was scared of saying the wrong thing again. After all, he could never imagine what she had been through or what she was about to go through – he wasn't about to pretend otherwise. Jane scratched her neck roughly, her pupils darting every which way before going back to the coffee. Her hair was wavy and naturally dark roots flowed into a muted blonde. She wore little make up other than around her eyes, which were dark and alluring. A silver nose ring was like a magnet to her fingers as she began.

Her story, starting from when she was hired as an intern for Young, was filled with extreme detail. She shook her head as if to reset when she found herself on a tangent. Gareth Young had found her on social media. She was, by every definition, an admirer. A hint of pride still broke through as Jane told Richard how her blogs and essays caught his eye and impressed him enough to hire her. As the relationship, both working and personal, grew, they would stay late in his office working on the wording of his announcements and press conferences. Sometimes they would slip in an obscure word and she would delight in watching him say it on live television – their little secret. Jane was honest about how and when their sex began, and why not? He was single and so was she. The trouble started when she ended it, believing her career to be on the verge of being written off as something she had sold her body for. "One day, I told him no." That word – no – was spoken devoid of meaning. She said it like a sigh. Jane had made it clear that it was over, but Gareth wasn't finished. What began with glancing touches on the shoulder and kisses excused as old habits quickly turned into something more sinister. Gareth Young would write lewd and inappropriate drafts of speeches and force her to add notes, glaring at her as she read over them. Jane, she assured Richard, was still in possession of these. One particularly hectic morning found them working alone in his flat. Jane swears she heard a snap as his expression changed and he lunged at her, desperate to ignore the work and 'let off steam.'

"He didn't rape me." She said, her eyes begging Richard to still take her seriously. "His hands went places and – but it wasn't... We didn't have sex."

Richard wanted to tell her that it didn't matter. That his intentions were clear and, even more so, were her objections. He wanted to comfort the lost and jobless woman sitting in front of him, suffering prolongingly at the hands of a man in power. A man that she was clearly in love with. In the end, he couldn't find the words. Anything on the tip of his tongue seemed empty and useless compared to what Jane had been put through. Her embarrassment at the assault not leading to rape, and the idea that if it did it would be more important, hurt him deeply. At that moment, he knew he would write Jane's story with as much input from her as he could gain. He would disregard his respect for the politician and his fear of the brick walls ready to be crashed into, because it was the absolute least he, or any other man, could do.

Jane's hand went limp in his as they said their goodbyes, agreeing to meet up again and record the interview. He had the feeling that it may never happen, that her pain and fragilities would take over. She had taken the first step of a steep climb – it would be much easier to turn back now.

But that didn't happen. Jane returned a week later more confident, a pattern that would form over the six months of them working together. All the while, Gareth Young was busy growing in popularity, confidence, and power.

6

Siestas – commonly used if you're either Spanish or rich and famous. The welcome party had wound down of its own accord, groups dispersing one after another until the staff felt it safe enough to clean up. Now it was time for a nap, or a few lines of cocaine, depending on which tent you poked your head into. The evening had that intriguing quality of either classiness or straight up debauchery. Only a simple thing had to change at a party for it to switch from one to the other. A particular song, a responsible adult having one drink more than usual or a lengthy spell of blistering sun – the inciting incident didn't matter, what mattered was that the rest of the party followed.

Hate them or love them, the celebrity circuit took a specific type of person to succeed. A perfect potion of arrogance but awareness that, in the grand scheme of things, you were disposable and could be disposed of for the cruelest of reasons. Up close, it wasn't hard to see the tenderness and fragility of any of these people, which was probably the reason that everyone was kept as far away as possible. Richard walked through the sparse crowd, keeping his eyes on any one thing or person for a short amount of time. He was aware he could look either judgmental or like a stalker – neither of which he wanted to be known for. It was easy to see cliques when you weren't a part of one, and there were many. He recognised a few faces he had written stories on in the past, almost all of which weren't very kind to the person in question. Ava had better have a good reason for inviting him, other than as a sacrificial member of the fourth estate. The wind had picked up a fair pace as if it was reacting to all of this tech and modernity intruding on the island where nature mostly ruled. The initial novelty of the camping arrangement had worn off quickly, and there were a few more whines and moans as time went on. Richard couldn't help thinking that it was organised at least partly for Ava's amusement. As far as he could gather, only a handful here were close friends. She was in that upper echelon of status where people generally wanted something from her, rarely the other way around. By all accounts, she was generous with her recommendations, and many had found their way up the ladder in her shadow. Maybe events like this were a sort of twisted interview process. If so, Richard couldn't help wondering what he was doing there. There was no question that she knew about the scandal he was the catalyst of – was it simply pity? There was nothing he disliked more than being felt sorry for.

Feeling the thoughts festering in the sheets of plastic surrounding him, he left his tent for some air. There were a few people sunbathing in what felt like the best weather of summer so far. The sort of day that would be talked about for years. A young woman covered her eyes to check if Richard was worth talking to, and apparently decided that he wasn't. He walked around the side of the country house towards the row of quad bikes. Touching the hard plastic framing the wheels, he wondered how fast you would have to drive it to reach the water from the cliffs.

"You ever been on one?" A voice, not long broken, came from behind him. Richard took a breath to get rid of the adrenalin and answered before turning round.

"I haven't actually. Not sure I'd trust myself to keep the wheels on the ground." Turning round, calm now, he was faced with a teenage boy.

"They're quite hard to flip over. Heavy." The young boy extended a hand. Richard noted the good manners as he accepted.

"Richard."

"Brad. Nice to meet you." Brad hadn't been taught to shake hands. It was limp and uncomfortable.

"You here to make sure nobody gets on these under the influence, Brad?" Richard was drawn to his eyes – blue and slightly shiny as if tears were never far away. Brad blushed at the assumption.

"Oh, no. I'm not working. I've just been on one before. I'm here as – I'm with my -"

"Bradley!" A woman who Richard knew to be Ava's assistant, Tara, rounded the corner and joined them. She took her sunglasses off as she reached the shade. "Jesus I thought I'd lost you."

"I'm here with my mum." Brad finished, and turned his gaze towards her. "I'm fine, I was just having a look around." He spoke at her with a slight resentment, but Tara's interests were elsewhere.

"You're Richard aren't you?"

"Dick, if you like." Richard replied, using his habit of putting himself down before others got the chance. He saw Brad stifle a snigger.

"That's what Ava calls you." Tara said with a smile of her own.

"I like to think of it as affectionate. Jury's out though. We haven't met, have we?" It was their turn to shake hands now. As he got closer, Richard could see that Tara had been working for Ava for so long that she had started to look like her, a bit like owners and their dogs. Her blonde hair was wavy and tugged back into a ponytail, probably for efficiency. Her eyes were behind oversized clear glasses, the lenses highlighting the same striking blue as Brad's. Her son was taller than she was, and probably had been for a few years now. Still, they both held themselves similarly – just on the edge of confidence but with clear flashes of insecurity.

"No, but I've heard a lot about you. I'm sorry about what you're going through. If it's any help I thought the story was quite brave." Her eyes and firm grip told Richard that she was being sincere. He smiled to thank her.

Tara seemed more grown up than Ava, which is probably why she was considered as absolutely vital to her. She had the air of someone who had to take control of her life at a young age, or who fell pregnant earlier than most, which seemed to be the case.

"What's it like working with Ava then?" Richard was careful to say 'with' and not 'for.' Tara's phone rang in her pocket. She smiled.

"That should tell you all you need to know. Come on, Bradley."

"I was thinking of taking one of these for a spin – he's welcome to come." Richard patted the quadbike, knowing that he wouldn't do anything stupid if he was forced into being the responsible adult. Tara considered it.

"Maybe tomorrow? Yes, tomorrow would be ideal."
Brad accepted it as if his plans were always put off until the next day. He waved as he followed Tara back towards the front of the house.

Tough life, Richard thought to himself. He was certain he would have grown up not wanting for anything, other than some friends and a bit of normality.

Richard's phone seemed to find the same spot of signal that Tara's had – it buzzed erratically, announcing plenty of messages and emails. Being off the grid was great until you remembered that it couldn't last forever. The communications were the same as they had been for the last week - requests for comment and notice of cancellation of upcoming work, sometimes from the same person. He hadn't figured out how he would move forward from this yet, still appreciating the comfort of the self-destructive phase too greatly. And yet, the glaring inevitability that he would have to address it one day was always there, hiding just poorly enough in the corner of his mind so he could see it. He thought of Tara, who seemed so in control. She wouldn't wallow from a setback or a scandal – it was her job to deal with those. A single mother and personal assistant, she not only had her own life to manage, but that of Brad's and Ava's. Three sets of drama, emotions and secrets all on her shoulders. Richard admired her. Wherever in the world his inspiration for redemption lay, he was almost certain it wasn't on this island. He decided against the quad bike, scared of what he would do.

Brad was used to watching his mother's heels clip clopping a few metres in front of him, or hearing them round a corner when he tried to steal a few moments to himself. *Bradley.* He was beginning to hate how she said that and the tone she took. High pitched and drawn out like a ghost in the night searching for a long-lost love. She walked as if she always had somewhere to be, which she did. He had considered running away many times. Thoughts of copying the cartoons he watched as a child with a rag tied to a stick slung over his shoulder grew into more serious plans as he matured. These days he would consider leaving once or twice a month at least. Tonight though, he was trapped. Worse still, the entire weekend was about Ava. Everything her mother ever did was about her, but he could usually tune out. Not today. He had thought since there was a party to plan that he might even be able to get some time alone, but she quickly saw to stopping that.

"Best behaviour tonight?" She posed it as a question, but it wasn't. Entering the house behind her, Brad dug his fingernails into his palms as deep as they would go. *Maybe if I start bleeding she'll notice I hate everything about our life* he thought. No, she doesn't notice anything unless it concerns Ava. He let his mind wander as he walked off into the room he had been assigned and his mother tended to Ava. Brad checked his phone for a signal. None - but he knew there wouldn't be any messages even if there was. He opened Instagram – it was logged in to the account his mum knew nothing about. A picture of a cartoon cat and the name *alpha_male666999* made sure that she would stay oblivious. The feed hadn't updated since they left the mainland, but a bit of maneuvering around the room finally found a connection. The posts refreshed – nothing he was interested in, of course. Instead, Brad went to the search bar and clicked the first suggested account. *Ava Hart Official.* He clicked the first picture – it had been taken with the island as a backdrop. Brad's fingers worked quickly. *Slut.* He posted the comment. A couple of taps and he was in the next account. *BetaBoi69* commented on the second latest picture, saying *Get out of the spotlight – nobody cares about you.* He was working at speed now. *GammaGamer225* told Ava and her followers that she ruins families. *DeltaDamien00* found a picture of her in a bikini and pointed out that she looked fat and disgusting. Finally, *EpsilonEddy1* pleaded with her in the comments section. *I'm going to kill myself because of you.* Brad dropped the phone, hoping deep inside that it would smash and his habit would be taken from him. It didn't. He grabbed at the roots of the haircut his mum had forced on him after a recommendation from Ava, pulling until his eyes watered. He shrugged off the pink hoodie she had picked for him and tugged at the neck of the polo shirt she had complimented. Everything was Ava, and it was getting dangerously cold in her shadow. Brad pressed his face against the window and slowed his breathing. He looked towards the intriguing, welcoming cliffs.

7

A bonfire had been lit to provide some ambience, but it had ended up giving off more of a tribal and tense vibe proving that the setting made no difference and the people within it would steer the mood. Churches could host a wedding one day and a funeral the next – the place didn't change but the atmosphere did. Thrusting out of the speakers, the bass drum loop gave the island a frenetic heartbeat. It wasn't hard to imagine a pair of influencers dropping their champagne and wrestling to assert some dominance. The loser would crouch and crawl away from the firelight, the winner taking centre stage and waiting for the next challenger. Richard decided that he had been staring into the flames for too long. He had been drawn away from the house and towards them – a different zone with a different theme. Ava was going all out. He was seeing most of the people there for the first time, confirming that the attendance numbers easily went into triple figures. The attempt in his head to name five people he would invite to a party of his own lasted less than a minute before he stopped himself, fearing depression. And yet, he probably knew Ava better than most here. They had drifted apart for sure, but the way they slipped so effortlessly back into the old dynamics told him that he could still read her well, and she him. One thing he would put money on was Ava making fun of the kinds of people she now mixed with, but what choice did she have really? Despite her maverick image, you couldn't be crowned the winner if you didn't play the game. So how much of it was a game and how much did she like these people? Or want their approval? As an atheist, he was closer to finding God than he was the answer to that but was convinced that there must be at least a handful here who she had made real connections with. People couldn't live without real connections – Richard knew because he was so lacking in them that sometimes it felt like he was gradually fading away. Why? Because he spent too much time doing exactly what he was doing in that moment – living in his head to the point of transcendence.

He gave his shoulders a quick shrug and took in what was around him rather than inside him. David the manager was skirting the area. For the second or third time, it was as if he and Richard had magnets on their chests pointing the wrong way. He was sure that the gulf between them would close at one point during the night, as it tended to when one person was avoiding another. What bothered him was the reason he was being avoided in the first place. Maybe it confirmed that David and Ava were an item at one point. An encounter with a lover's ex, no matter how many moons ago they came from, was something many would choose to not take part in. From the way he walked and talked, Richard was struggling to imagine any situation that David wouldn't swagger into and take control of. His toned body was on show, undoubtedly gained by hours in the gym but aided quite a bit by an extreme slim fit fashion line and below average height. His thick hands found their way onto whoever he was talking to – a shoulder, a hip, sometimes even a cheek like he was a mob boss or a clingy grandmother. If they were having a silent battle of who was more comfortable - which they were, Richard decided – David was winning. He floated in and out of conversations and always left to a laugh or a playful raising of the eyebrows. Richard, on the other hand, was staring at the fire again like a troubled child whose only friend at school was the janitor. The difference was that people wanted to talk to David, or be seen doing so. Richard's quick search online earlier that day showed that he carried a serious amount of clout in the celebrity world – a proven star maker.

"Your face is starting to melt." A young man sidled up beside him and pointed to his bulging eye. Richard smiled.

"Good one." He said, extending his hand. "I'm Richard."
The young man accepted it with a hint of sarcasm and faux formality. Handshakes were out of fashion apparently.

"Devin." He said. "Have the fights started already?"

"I brought this one with me actually." Richard said, signalling to his eye. "Do you expect there to be fights?"

"Please. Almost certainly."
Richard tried to place Devin but failed, making him feel much older than he rightfully should.

"Looking to get a minute with David, are you?" Devin had a Scottish accent – one of the first Richard had heard on the island after himself and Ava. His trousers were gold and his paisley patterned shirt had only the bottom button fastened, exposing a hairless and tanned chest. He seemed as Scottish as the Pope.

"Is it that obvious?" Richard asked, going into super undercover investigative journalist mode.

"Either that or you're going to attack him. The whole flames dancing on the face while you stare at someone isn't a great look."

Richard smiled at Devin's way with words once again.

"I've just heard how good he is at what he does."

"You want him to represent you?" Devin asked with a slow smile creeping in. Richard shrugged but looked open to the idea. A white lie.

"You've got a bit too much Y chromosome to be considered."

"He only deals with women?" Richard didn't sound surprised.

"He's known for it."

"Why?"

"Depends who you ask."

"What if I asked you?" Richard said. Devin smiled and sipped a bright cocktail.

"Oh, I don't know. Short guy - a power thing? He's straight, so there's that. Maybe he didn't have much luck with the girls when he was younger. Maybe he just knows they're more marketable, or that there's a bigger pool to choose from."

"I'm sure one of them is right. What do you do?"

"Blogger." Devin said as he bopped his head along with the bass. "You?"

"Journalist."

"Oh. Sorry about the whole putting you out of business thing."

"That's okay – we probably deserve it. You write anything I'd be interested in?"

"Check me out – Devin's Diary. What about you?"

"Probably not." Richard admitted. Devin smiled.

"I'm gonna do a lap. Nice to meet you. Sparks flew et cetera." Devin nodded to the fire before swaying out of Richard's space and into someone else's.

Richard pulled up the website on his phone. It was bright with bold text and huge areas to click on that took you from story to story, linked with keywords, names and dates. Compared to a mainstream news website, it was infinitely better. No ads, no auto-playing videos, no scrolling issues and no typos. Richard felt a bit embarrassed for his industry, which had spectacularly fumbled the transition to digital, holding the door open for people like his new friend. Devin wrote as he spoke, and clearly knew his audience as well as how to keep them there. The headlines were typically intriguing, even for Richard who either didn't know the people they concerned or didn't care about them. Until he scrolled by Ava. A video interview from a few weeks ago. He bookmarked the page and pocketed his phone. He'd hopefully get up to speed with how Ava had changed by watching it in the privacy of his tent later. In fact, he felt confident he would after finding out how switched on Devin was. Power was the first thing he attributed to David's need to work with women, and Richard figured that he was spot on.

As he pondered it, David was talking to a young woman and giving her tips on her posture. His hands shifted her stance and her body like someone at a pottery wheel. Richard leant closer to the fire and used it to light a cigarette, feeling the heat on his wound and keeping his eyes on Ava's manager through the orange blaze. He took a draw and walked away, leaving the tribes behind.

David kept an eye on Richard, not listening to the girl in front of him because he was an expert at tuning unnecessary noise out. He was disappointed that Richard hadn't approached him, because he had his opening line cocked and loaded. *I've worked too hard to know who you are.* He'd say with a smile. It was one he said to guys quite often to put them in their place, but a quick recce of the area told him that he hadn't used it on anybody here and that it would look spontaneous. As usual, he was ten steps ahead of any scenario that might present itself which, as far as he was concerned, was the only way to succeed in life. Make a habit of falling into situations you can't control and you'll never catch your grip again.

"So what do you think?" Her voice was deep – startlingly so considering her tiny frame. David noted it as a potential selling point and handed her a thick business card. Unlike others, he didn't give them out to anybody. The young woman took it with the care she would a train ticket to paradise. She made her best attempt at walking off casually. David watched her go – something he always made sure to do. He liked being in control. The job had many perks and he wasn't for missing any of them, especially as it likely wouldn't last forever. The culture outside of the industry had moved at a quicker pace than the industry itself. People looking in thought their constant screeching for equality was working, and it was, but slowly. At this point he could still sideline some talent if she was pregnant, or in that awkward age between teenager and mature woman. There wouldn't be any complaints if he lost it at someone for turning up late or unprepared, or sacked someone for being incompetent. He could do what he always did, but change was creeping in. David would check his actions daily unless he knew he could cover himself, although this was getting much harder with journalists like Richard Dickson weaselling around. A self-righteous wet wipe of a man, whose hypocrisy was even greater than each and every one of these celebrities. Still, he was to be worried about, if only because he was a wounded animal whose next move could either be the end or a second chance.

Someone offered him a drink, but he declined. It was something he had learned from Ava – sparkling water and ice between every drink set a slow pace. David couldn't count the amount of people on the island who would be legless before the sun set. Loose lips and careless encounters, he thought. Not him, and not Ava. The fact that she rarely celebrated her life, achievements or birthdays made him weary that that night may be the one for her to go wild. He had seen her drunk on only a handful of occasions, and it wasn't nice. Not only that, but it could potentially spell disaster for him. She knew more about him than his own mother. Things that would shock and disturb people, and back him into the corner that he had fought his entire career to avoid. There were plenty here to listen, too – not least Richard Dickson. Bloggers, gossips and enemies bobbing above the surface like crocodiles waiting for a carcass to be thrown their way. David relished a fight, in fact he was known for it. This was no different. The longest battle of his life – staying on top, away from the snapping jaws of the culture.

8

His finger hovered over the screen ready to press play. Why wouldn't he just walk the hundred metres to speak to Ava and hear her story from the source? Part of him was embarrassed that he hadn't kept up to date with what she was doing, who she was seeing and what kind of person she was. Another part thought that she may not be as honest with him as she once would have been. Both urged him to start the video, so he did.

Devin's studio was as bright as he seemed to be – contrasting pinks and greens with plants and books sparsely dotted around. Ava shared the same sofa as him – an old technique to get the interviewee to open up – and their bodies were angled towards one another.

"Ava Hart – thank you for finally coming on. You don't do many interviews these days do you? Why is that?" Devin got straight into it even before Ava had finished her slight nod to say hello. She took her cue as if she had been provided with the questions beforehand, although Richard was almost certain that Devin had a few to surprise her with.

"We live in a world now that I can speak directly to my audience. I can answer their questions live, respond to their messages, give them my unfiltered thoughts – why would I do it any other way?"

"Have you had problems with your words being taken out of context in the past?"

"Show me someone who sits here and says they haven't and I'll show you a liar." Ava and Devin shared a smile.

"Honey, there will be none of that here. We're just a vessel for you to reach the masses."

"Well that's good to hear. Thanks for having me." Ava's public accent was what Richard would call 'accessible Scottish' – she held onto the inflections and tones of her home country but made sure she was eloquent and always easy to understand.

"When did you realise you wanted to become famous?" Devin asked, sipping a coffee.

"I never wanted to be famous – it just happened to be a nice bonus that came with entertaining people, or making them smile." It was clear that she had been well trained to not put a foot wrong in these types of interviews. It was a shame really – Richard remembered interviewing people at the start of his career and marveling at them not carefully considering their answers before providing them. It was rare to leave an interview without something that could be considered a bombshell. Now, fronted by Ava, the subjects knew all too well that one word or hint out of place would be picked apart and could lead to their downfall. It drove readers to gossip sites and forums, because they knew nothing juicy would come from the horse's mouth. That's when the smart interviewees started to calculate and script what they would say, ultimately providing an answer that accidentally hinted to some drama or news. Of course, it was far from unintentional.

"You're the perfect example of an independent woman, aren't you?"

"Oh you wouldn't say that if you seen the amount of people who help with everything I do, Devin – they're some of the brightest people in the industry."

"Don't be coy, you know what I mean – you've been in the spotlight for over 10 years and we've only ever heard whisperings about a partner. You haven't been pictured with anyone, or spotted on a date. You must agree that's quite unusual in the times we live in?"

"Why is it unusual?"

"I'm not sure why it is – but I'm sure that it is." Devin said. Ava smiled, enjoying the verbal spar, or at least appearing to.

"Okay, agreed. Do you really think after years of keeping my private life private that I would throw it all away in a moment? I like you Devin, but you're smarter than that."

"Okay how about instead of asking if you have someone special in your life, I'll ask why you want to keep it a secret either way? Is it a way for appealing to single fans and coupled up ones at the same time?"

"I wish I was as smart as that."

"I think we both know that you are."

"You're not letting me off the hook here are you?" Ava, despite her word, was still in control.

"Not until you give me something." Devin smiled and it was returned, although with a bit less enthusiasm this time. Was it an act Ava was in on? Richard, to his embarrassment, couldn't tell anymore. She took a long pause as Devin's eyes remained on hers. This is how he earned a living.

"Love is circumstantial, isn't it? To fall in love with someone, you have to know them, and to know them you have to be around them. It's why so many people meet in the office or at school – they're around a person enough to give love a chance." Ava paused again. Devin looked pleased so far, but didn't miss a beat when it came to urging her to be more specific.

"So how does that apply to you?" He asked.

"Well the problem is a mix of things. I was hurt when I was young, and now I'm not around anybody enough to give love a chance."

"So there's been nobody over the years?"

"I wouldn't say that – just no love."

Devin took his time, but eventually accepted that he wouldn't be getting anything more on this subject. He faced the camera, which startled Richard slightly and made him feel exposed.

"A word from out sponsors." He squeezed Ava's hand as the video cut to an advert.

She had been hurt when she was young. Richard thought. He didn't know whether to feel sympathy or guilt – could it have been him? But she had been the one doing the hurting, not the other way around, at least in his head. He swiped the video away, promising himself that any other questions he had about Ava he would ask her himself. He lit a cigarette and lay back, ignoring the flammable warnings on the tent surrounding him.

"Just the man I was looking for." Paul De Rossi felt the strong palm on his shoulder and knew that the man looking for him was the very same one he had been avoiding.

"David – how are you?" He replied. The journalist and manager shook hands.

"How am I? Insulted that my favourite journo has been so elusive recently."

"I'm always around when there's a story, you know that." Paul said. They shared the fakest of smiles.

"And what's the story today?" David asked.

"I'm here as a guest, remember?"

"I'd believe you if I didn't know how much of a sleazeball you were." David winked. De Rossi thought *it takes one to know one* but didn't have the guts to say it. Ava Hart's manager – and manager of many other young stars for that matter – was famous for his temper. A simple joke could be taken as the ultimate insult. The problem was you never really know what mood you'd catch him in, and that unpredictability was behind the fear that most in the industry experienced around him.

"Well to be a guest at the *biggest and best* celebration of the year that went *without any drama* is an honour, I'm sure."

De Rossi understood the message – it was to be the headline he would use if he wanted to keep the benefits of acquaintance with David Morgan.

"Agreed." He said, wondering if there would be a day where he would stand up to the industry forces that steered him. Because of course, David was far from the only one. *In too deep.* he thought.

"What do you know about that Dick, Dickson?" David asked, sipping what looked like water.

"Almost finished. Did you read the Gareth Young story?"

"I did. I believed him as well, but that stays between us."

"Oh me too, but that doesn't really matter does it?" De Rossi admitted.

"Not really. So you don't think he's looking to bounce back?"

"He'd be naïve to try and do it with Ava, and for as long as I've known him he isn't naïve. Although I was surprised to see him on the list."

"Me too. Apparently they had some silly high school romance. Maybe you remember him?" David asked.

"Not me. Was he around in the beginning?"

"She would speak about him now and then, but not for long." He looked annoyed that De Rossi had nothing to offer.

The two of them had been instrumental in Ava Hart's career from the very start. David as an up-and-coming manager got his claws into her early, spotting the potential and warning her of the vultures in the industry. De Rossi, who had graced the newsroom only a handful of times, was tasked with writing the story of the girl who had been scouted at a school talent show. At the time he cursed his new editor for giving him a 'non-event' assignment. How wrong that turned out to be.

"Anyway, we've got a job to protect her, you and I." David continued. Another one of his old tricks – treat whoever he's using as a teammate. De Rossi hated being on his side, but it was true – he had protected Ava in the past by catching and killing stories, or distracting the masses with something new. Why? Because David was a gatekeeper to more stories, content and scoops. At certain points over the years, Paul had to admit that information provided by David's camp had saved him from redundancy and debt. Because of that, his dance with the devil was to last an eternity.

"Two things I need from you. Find out what his game is, and convince him to stop it. Good lad." David didn't need to wait for a confirmation. After another strong hand on the shoulder, he left Paul De Rossi feeling dirty, which was far from a new state for him to be in.

David Morgan, now there's a story he thought. But no, he was far too much of a coward to do that. A well-trained dog who would sit in the road and be hit by a car if his owner had told him to stay.

9

"He was wandering around like a lost puppy." Tara was fastening Ava's red dress at the shoulders.

"Yep, that's Richard." She dropped her hair back down when the knot was tied tightly across her back.

"And what's he doing here again? You've not mentioned him in years."

"God you sound just like him – what if I just wanted to re-ignite an old friendship?" Ava saw Tara's arched eyebrow in the mirror and conceded defeat. "You're impossible to lie to. I just felt like he could use a break."

"And you're the one to give him it?" Tara asked.

"Maybe I will be." Ava answered, short enough to let her know that the conversation should move on. Tara didn't take the hint.

"He was talking to Bradley." Tara said. Ava turned to face her at this.

"I love that you're so protective of him, but you can trust Richard. I'm sure of it."

"He's not – you know – is he?"

"Let's not talk about that now, T." Ava's look was ice cold, and Tara knew not to press the matter.

"So I can trust him – what about everyone else out there?" Tara gestured towards the balcony.

"Them? Maybe not so much. Better make sure he doesn't end up in a tent with a few girls tonight." Ava laughed and Tara joined in, albeit nervously.

Ava loved the moments of laughter they shared, fleeting but still there after all these tough years. She moved towards the balcony causing her hair to fall from Tara's hands as she was putting it up. The sun was like a spotlight on Ava, and she noticed some her guests looking up towards her. Some waved or raised their glasses, some turned back to their friends and undoubtedly began to talk about her. Let them talk, she thought, she was used to that. The years she had spent reading her story told in the words of others had given her an armour that not many could claim to have. It was almost time to tell it her way, with the help of a few people and the threats of others. The fact that they had all shown up was a good sign – the first battle won.

In the small crowd, Ava spotted Hayley – the woman the press had branded her nemesis many years ago. Amongst the sea of Americans in their world, the two of them had come up in the United Kingdom. The fact that this made them rivals and not allies had baffled Ava in the beginning, but Hayley seemed to be content with the dynamic, capitalising on the drama at every available opportunity. Side by side, they could be sisters, and they had squabbled like them in the past. Last year, Hayley had posted a series of videos *exposing* Ava and her ways with people – amongst her claims were mistreatment of staff, and cruel behaviour towards people she deemed beneath her. In the fallout, David, their mutual manager, dropped Hayley as a client in favour of his longer relationship with Ava. She had long buried the ill feelings towards the whole situation, and the fact that Hayley had accepted the invite here made her think that she had done the same. As she had to do at many points in her life, she reminded herself that things were often more complicated than they seemed.

The music was back on but reduced now to background noise. Richard decided to decline the drink on the tray in front of him. He accepted a glass full of ice to hold against his eye instead. The swelling hadn't gone down enough to stop people asking about it, but he knew that they would have probably ignored him completely otherwise so was quite thankful for the talking point. Since his younger years he had been known for listening intently and not offering much in return. He had been called guarded, quiet, and even strange from time to time. The real reason behind how he acted was less curiosity and more an urge to never look inwardly – if he was processing other people's problems and choices then he had no time to address his own. If pushed on it, he supposed that his mother's death had played a part in how he was as well. Often he couldn't shake the feeling that people weren't showing him full pictures, just corners and segments of them. Of course, that was normal, especially now. Almost everybody he was sharing the island with was a master of angles – filtering out the negative and projecting perfection. As Richard watched people get ready for the evening's party, he saw the complete opposite to himself – self obsession to the extreme. If his lack of interest in himself was a form of mental malnourishment, almost everybody else here was clinically obese. Most of the young women around him had fallen in love with the camera, and gazed at themselves through the lens of their phones. Richard wondered how long it had taken for them to like what they saw, or if they even really did at all. That was the problem with filters and angles – use them enough and they become a part of you. He had no doubt that if people laid themselves bare more often, society would be a less anxious and cagey beast. Of course, he was as guilty as the rest for not doing this, just in different ways.

"Do I recognise you, son?" An accent from the north of England somewhere, with the inflections to suggest that they had grown up working class but made their way upwards, picking up some posh traits along the way. Richard looked up at the man – maybe 50 years old, about six five with a presidential cut that added another couple of inches. There were plenty of people in the world whom he would resent for calling him son. This man wasn't one of them. Richard knew exactly who he was.

"I'm not sure, but I could make a guess at you." He extended a hand which was accepted, and engulfed, by Herbert, the man who had discovered Ava at their school all those years ago. "I was in Ava's class the day that you and your team ran the auditions." Richard said. Herbert offered an empty smile, but wasn't satisfied that it was why he recognised Richard. Even so, he left it.

"Changed days now." Herbert motioned with his glass towards the group of people who had come here for the star of the show. "I knew this was what she was destined for though. Nothing was stopping her."

"Still in the game of finding the next big thing?" Richard asked.

"With less success." Herbert nodded – a man longing for the old days. He had tired eyes and looked kind. Coupled with his imposing physicality, he was the sort of person you would trust your career with.

"Still, it must be a proud moment for you – seeing this." Richard said as he looked out onto the glamour that was all for Ava.

"I knew early on that Ava would go on to big things. She showed incredible drive." He smiled to show that he was indeed proud.

"What do you think's next for her?" Richard had been wondering this himself. From the moment they had been reunited he had sensed that she had a plan forming in her head.

"You're a journalist aren't you? That's where I know you from?"

"Guilty. But this is off the record – I'm here as an old friend, just like you." Richard replied.

Herbert studied him for a moment.

"I'd like to see her go out on top. I've seen too many outstay their welcome and ruin what they've built."

A group of young women passed them and waved. "Hi Herb!" came the chorus. He smiled and waved.

"You seem like someone they look up to." Richard told him.

"I like to think so – it's a damn shame that the same can't be said about more people."

"Nasty business?" Richard already knew the answer.

"You have no idea, son." Herb's face wrinkled at the thought, the lines on his forehead telling tales of a career witnessing bullying and injustice.

"Ever think about calling it a day yourself?"

"These people need a good guy – maybe I will when I'm sure that the next one has come along." Herb said. Richard got the hint that today wasn't the day Herbert would be blowing the whistle on the bad guys, so he didn't ask anything further.

"I was hoping you two would meet." Ava's voice carried its way from behind them and they both turned to see her. She wasn't quite ready for the party, but even that was enough to make most people stare. Herbert extended his arm, a warm and genuine smile forming on his face. Richard could be sure that his eyes were getting teary.

"Darling." He said as Ava accepted the embrace. She smiled, but didn't quite emulate his nostalgia – her years had been filled with new, more important people.

"Richard, do you remember Herb?" She asked. He nodded. "Richard and I were something of an item at the time you whisked me away." She said, addressing Herbert now.

"Ahh, sorry about that, son." Herb smiled again, still with his hands on Ava's shoulders as if he had caught the past and didn't want to let go.

"Can we catch up later?" Ava asked Herbert, who nodded, finally noticing that he was being a bit sentimental and releasing Ava. He patted Richard on the shoulder and wandered into the crowd.

"Nice guy." Richard said, imagining that those had been the words spoken hundreds of times as Herbert exited rooms.

"The reason this all started." Ava said with a confident smile, turning to walk and assuming he would follow. He did.

10

They weren't on a path, but Ava seemed to know where they were going. The house and the beginnings of the party were getting smaller in the distance as they headed towards the sunset.

"Looking forward to tonight?" Richard asked, having waited long enough for her to speak. She simply nodded. They covered a bit more distance before Richard stopped and looked at her.

"Is this where you tell me why I'm here?"

Ava stopped too and smiled. Anybody who had watched her on their screens for years could never be disappointed at the real thing – Richard supposed that the main source of attraction was more how she acted and how secure she was rather than her attributes. *You could've been with her through it all.* He told himself. Then again, wasn't that wishful thinking? Had she not ended it in high school to go and become a star, surely the time would have come a year or two later. He was too cynical, too guarded and too selfish to be with someone so confident and ambitious. These feelings sent him back to when they broke up, and how childishly he had acted.

"I know we've never been good at the whole deep conversation thing – but how are you?" She asked.

Richard searched for a joke or a playful insult on the horizon, but only concern showed on Ava's face now. She had brought him here to support him. To find out if he was coping with the scandal, and maybe if she could help. He felt disappointed. Not by the fact that Ava was doing this, but because he had never done the same. Decades of friendship and he had never once reached out in the way she was doing now. As soon as it was his career on the line, and his mental health, Ava was there.

The least he could do was give her a proper answer, but what he wanted to say had been something he had struggled to put into words over the last month. He felt vulnerable, scared even. He wanted to tell her about the fleeting thoughts of suicide, but something inside put a halt to that.

"I was trusted with something important, and I fumbled it. You spend your life thinking about how you'll handle certain situations, preparing yourself and telling yourself that you can do it. Then, the time comes and you fuck it up." Richard said.

"You didn't fumble anything, it was knocked out of your hands. How's the girl?"

"She's not answering my calls." It was a source of extreme guilt for Richard that Jane had trusted him and now was in hiding, or worse, being silenced. Ava considered it for a minute. As she looked out towards the horizon she looked angry, resolute.

"Before you ask, there's nothing you can do." Richard said. She was about to protest. "Well, I'm sure there is. It's just, I need to fix this myself."

"And how's that going?" Ava shot a cruel glance at his eye injury.

"Slowly." He admitted.

"I've met a hundred journalists – know why you're different?"

"They were good?" Richard said quickly. Ava laughed at this.

"No. You give a shit, and you'll write what you see no matter if you like it or not, or it makes life hard for you." Richard thanked her with a smile. "You'll come back from this – just wait and see. And then one day you can tell my story?" She posed it as a question.

"I'm not sure I'd do it justice." He looked around the island.

"I think you'd be surprised." She teased.

"What about Paul De Rossi – I see he was on the guest list?" Richard knew that De Rossi had covered Ava's entire career, but he didn't know how mutual the obsession was.

"I could tell you some stories about him for a change." She paused to think for a moment, and then looked back towards the house. "In fact, can we meet later? It'll be like old times.

Midnight?"

Richard nodded. In high school, they had lived only a few streets apart. After the various drunken parties - the first of their lives and nothing like this one – they always walked home together, holding onto one another for balance and dissecting the teenage dramas that seemed so important back then. The park that they had sat in hosted arguments, flirtations and deep conversations. The two of them had forgotten more from those nights than they had remembered, but the feeling of each other's company on a cold, dark and silent night would never leave them. Richard felt something in his stomach when he realised they would be doing it once more after all of those years apart. It took him a second to recognise the feeling as excitement – all that had been there recently was anxiety.

"Where do you go?" Ava asked, snapping him out of his trance. All he could offer was a noise, prompting her to repeat herself. "You drift off in the middle of conversations – always have."

"Yeah a lot of people say that. I like to think it makes me look a bit mysterious. Truth is I can't really concentrate on too many things at once." Richard admitted.

"Nice to know I was second string to whatever's in your head."

"It was you, just the old you."

Ava considered this for a second. She pushed her hair behind one ear, but the wind blew it straight back into place.

"You think I've changed that much?"

"Everyone does." He shrugged.

"Why?" She asked.

"You mean why does everyone change? We grow up, things happen that force us to."

"Is that what happened to the girl you wrote about?"

Richard nodded, wondering if one day when someone mentioned Jane the lump in his throat wouldn't come. Ava was doing everything she could to meet his eyes, but they darted between points on the ground.

"When she told you – how was she?" Ava continued.

"You mean like was she relieved?" He replied, finally giving in and looking at Ava. She nodded. "I don't think so. Like I said, it had already changed her."

Ava wanted to help, that much was clear to Richard. He sensed that it was a mix of loyalty to him and sorrow for Jane. She couldn't though, and they both knew it. Nobody but Jane could alter the course of how things were going now, and Richard wouldn't blame her for holding onto any strength or hope she had left.

"Things have a funny way of getting back on track. You'll see." Ava said. Richard accepted the empty gesture with an empty smile. Her phone buzzed, and then again, and again. A rare pocket of signal meaning all the early birthday wishes were coming in at once.

"Better get back. Are you looking forward to the party?" She asked as they turned on their heels and headed for the house.

"Would you find it rude if I said no?"

Ava laughed, picking her mood back up as she neared her guests.

"Maybe you'll find some inspiration for your next story. I'd be interested to read your thoughts on some of these people." She said it with just enough spite, as if it was a serious message masked as a joke.

"Any one in particular?" He asked.
Ava picked up the pace, her body flowing into the rhythm like the rough terrain was a catwalk.

"Now that would ruin the game." She told him.

They walked in silence. The atmosphere was starting to taste toxic. Ava had stories to tell, the girls on the train had shown disdain for most of the guests and Herbert alluded to the industry's dark side. If this was a party, Richard wasn't sure they were for him anymore. His family had always said that he was an old soul – that he acted ten years older than he was. He tended to agree with the assessment. A near 50 year old trapped in a 35 year old's body. Cynical, impatient, brooding, secretive. While everyone around him was doing everything that they could to be younger again, he was waiting for the days that his personality would match him physically. He had told Ava that they were all forced to grow up as a consequence of something. She had been kind not to bring up the event that had changed him, which she and everyone who knew him in his younger years was well aware of.

11

"Richard, you're in charge."

The words from his mother still rang in his ears 24 years on. Not that anyone blamed him for what was to come. Mary, his younger sister by a year or so, didn't look like she was on the verge of adolescence. Her need to carry toys and sleep with the light on was, at the time, worrying their parents more and more. If she wet the bed, which wasn't rare, Richard helped her clean up in the hope that they wouldn't notice. She had done it the night before the day that changed him forever.

They were at the park, the very same where years later Richard would fall deeply for Ava in the tragic way teenage boys do. Despite it being small, a seemingly infinite number of the local kids could squeeze in between the rainbow-painted railings to play on the wood chips. Richard was towards the edge, kicking his ball off the metal in a pattern that was mesmerizing. *Ten. Eleven. Twelve.* He counted as he went. He was in charge. A quick glance over his shoulder meant he could check on Mary and still keep the rhythm going. He was on the way to a personal record. *Thirteen. Fourteen. Fifteen.* She was playing at the gate, burying a toy neck deep in the bark. As long as she didn't go outside of fence he could keep playing. *Sixteen. Seventeen. Eighteen.* Mary was a metre outside the park now, but still within touching distance of the railings. She was getting a toy and acting that it was on its way to save the other one. He nearly messed up there, misjudging an angled bounce. Back under control now. *Nineteen. Twenty. Twenty one.* Nothing to worry about. Mary was still there. Busy road, responsible people driving by not too fast. Close to the record now. *Twenty two. Twenty three. Twenty four.*

His leg was getting sore, but he couldn't switch to his left. It was useless. White van pulling up now. His dad had a white van. All under control. *Twenty five. Twenty six.* A scream like he'd never heard before, not even in the films. Mary's scream. He turned around and felt the ball bounce off his shin. Mary, held by her pigtails by two hands. Two hairy hands, no face, dragging her into the van. Richard's legs didn't work right away, despite his brain telling them to move. The door had slammed shut by then, muffling the scream but not drowning it out completely. *Mary* he screamed. *Mary. Mary. Mary.* Until the van had rounded the corner. Other kids were crying. So was he now. *Come back.* He shouted at the top of his voice. *Bring my sister back.* His words had done nothing.

Just like Richard, his parents were never the same again. They tried to be, but the grief battered them out of all recognition. It seemed like the whole of Glasgow searched nightly for Mary. To his young mind, this went on every night for a year. In reality it was less than a week until Mary's body was found, mangled, abused and tampered with in woods on the other side of the city. On the night they received the news, Richard's mum had held him for 5 or 6 hours straight without letting go. He remembered seeing the handprints on his back in the bathroom mirror where he watched himself cry and used every swear word that he knew to berate himself. But people were kind – if they had thought Richard was at fault, they did a stellar job of hiding it. In fact, he got twice the attention, gaining Mary's share. For the benefit of his mum and dad, he acted normal while knowing deep down that he never would be again. Years later he would realise that they were doing the same. In the months that followed her death, he would sleep with the toy that Mary had buried at the park. Some nights he would force himself to wet the bed, cleaning it up and talking to Mary as he did so. *Don't worry* he'd tell her. *I'll sort it out. It'll all be okay.*

After that initial period of childish grieving, Richard was grown. He understood that the world was a cruel place with crueler people. In his later school years, some days he would lead a normal life with normal teenage problems. He'd rejoice in something like a test or a fall out with a friend affecting him, almost searching out stress because anything was better than his mind reverting back to Mary's face as she was dragged from him. As years went on, he drifted away from the area he grew up in and the people in its orbit. Every interaction, relationship and friendship was framed by his tragedy. More often than not it wasn't brought to the surface, but he knew that it was affecting people's judgement of him and he hated it. Mary's death affected every decision he made. He studied journalism to tell people's stories and avoid telling his own. He found himself leaving himself open to dangerous situations, willing something to happen so he could act differently and, maybe, redeem himself. Her rapist and murderer had been caught quickly by the police. From what he overheard, it was a spontaneous act by a deranged man. Richard's mother had made him swear that he would never try to look into the animal. Throughout his life he was loose with alcohol, cigarettes and sex, but the one thing he remained in control of was not breaking that promise. When she died of the cancer, Richard and his Dad both wanted to open up to each other. Unfortunately, the emotional energy and woman's encouragement that they needed was gone for good. Instead, they visited and conversed pointlessly to fill the silence. To Richard, it looked like his dad had been rotting from the inside ever since Mary died, and the pace accelerated when Mum was gone too. To his dad, he probably looked the same. He often wondered how much of the turmoil that they each put themselves through every day could be fixed by a simple conversation or hug. He would stay wondering.

He wondered too what Mary would be like had she been alive with him, grown up with him and supported him. The Mary he had crafted in his head was perfect, of course. Sometimes on particularly rainy days, he would scald himself like he did in the mirror as a child. Of course she wouldn't be perfect. Just like him, she would have made mistakes and gone down the wrong paths. On brighter days, Mary was perfect again. His guiding light. Beautiful Mary was what every happy song was about. She was the reason behind any days he woke up smiling. She kept him alive, because despite the world testing him, he couldn't let her go again. Not only that, but he wanted to show her that good things could happen, and that bad people could be stopped. It just took time and persistence, like kicking the ball against the fence. *Twenty seven. Twenty eight. Twenty nine.*

12

Today you are the strongest you have ever been and you know more than you ever have.

The motivational slogan was projected onto one side of the island's house. Some people scoffed at it, others complimented it, but it made everyone think.

"Just between you and me, I've no idea why she invited me." Hayley, a social media influencer turned model, said for the eighth time of the evening. Amongst the smiles and nods of the head towards whoever was talking to her, she glanced to the balcony that she was certain would be the stage for Ava's grand entrance. How cliché – reenacting Romeo and Juliet. She was telling everybody here that they should love her without actually saying it. Hayley had always thought Juliet seemed like a bit of a bitch anyway. She had dressed down for the evening, wearing an oversized t-shirt with big boots. If she had come glamorous, people would compare and contrast her with the birthday girl. Don't even give them the chance, she thought. Plus, if she looked better than her in her casual clothes that would be a gut punch hard to recover from. Hayley's dark hair was tied up with a fringe bouncing with her movements. Bangs she called them, because she was trying to break into America just now. Just a touch of glitter on her bronzed skin – more like a supernatural being than a child who got into the craft box. Nobody had to tell her that she looked good, but they did anyway.

"So what was the beef?" Three girls from the US were standing talking to her. They had moved in a group all night like weaker animals would in the wild. *Beef*. Hayley made a mental note to start saying that instead of feud.

"We had the same manager. I was so fine with it. So fine. But he was like weirdly obsessed with her. I guess she told him to get rid of me." Hayley said with a shrug of the shoulders and a sip of her cocktail. Her audience of three gasped as if they were on the first passenger flight to Mars.

"No way. Scandal." The blonde one said. The brunette and redhead nodded.

"Everything happens for a reason." Hayley said, prompting more nods and smiles. Motivational quotes had been her bread and butter – it was amazing the followers you could get from re-cycling bullshit positivities. Personally, she didn't believe one of them, but nobody had to know that.

"I'm going to do a lap, ladies. It was so nice to meet you – I'll follow you." She said, waved and spun to see who else was worth her precious time. She knew there were two journalists in attendance and considered introducing herself. But to which one? The fat Italian one was tabloid, and he'd probably follow her around like a puppy. Could be fun. The other took him-self more seriously – wrote about *things that matter.* That didn't make any difference, they were both still part of an industry that was dying a very public death. He was standing alone, as he had been most of the day. As she clenched her straw between her teeth, she noticed eyes being drawn upwards. She turned back to see Ava on the balcony. Typical, Hayley thought. The music switched tracks to suit Ava's slow motion walk to the edge. God this was *so* typical. Ava waved, and Hayley smiled along with everyone else. Don't let them see your resentment, she told her-self. Theirs was a battle of pretending they didn't matter to each other. Still, Hayley had plans for Ava. Of course, there was room at the top for both of them, but that's not how she worked. Much more satisfying to step on heads on your way up than a stair-case. *Second place is just the first to lose.* Maybe there was a motiv-ational quote she agreed with after all.

The bass was booming and vibrating the blades of grass as Richard changed his shirt. He was only doing it because he thought the other guests might notice if he hadn't. He cursed the fact that he had brought three the same colour and style. No point in doing it at all really, but at least the fresh one didn't have blood on it. Ava had been fashionably late to her own party, which made her entrance all the better. There was something about her that made him see her actions as confidence rather than arrogance. If anybody else had unveiled themselves on a balcony as she just had, he would scoff and immediately take a dislike to them. But not Ava - why was that? Maybe, he thought, it was because he knew deep down she was a good person. Maybe knowing her before her stardom was a sort of internal claim to fame. Either way, she apparently could do no wrong in his eyes, which wasn't a good position for a journalist to take.

It amazed him how the venue could stay constant with the atmosphere changing with the time of day – the guests were now drinking and dancing two feet away from where they brushed their teeth that morning, or worked out a couple of hours ago. It was a hot, almost humid evening and when the wind blew it was welcome. As the sun continued to set, its job was taken up by LED and strobe lights, dotted around strategic-ally to make sure there was still privacy if a couple sought it. He was sure plenty would over the course of the night. For Rich-ard, the party was just a caveat before his midnight meeting. His cynicism sat on his shoulder, piping up every time he con-sidered joining a conversation or activity and convincing him against it. For that reason, he still stood on the patch of grass directly outside his tent like an astronaut taking cautious first steps from the vessel. Just on the fringes of the party like he had been for years. What had happened to the extroverted student who would play pool with strangers and talk the ear off anybody who would listen? His eye started hurting again, the alcohol and painkillers wearing off. He shouldn't take any more tablets, but drinking would still be acceptable.

As if by telepathy, a waiter brandished a tray of drinks in front of him, holding it just far enough away so he would need to take a step closer to the glee. He did. Being confident was his greatest trick – he had known that for a long time. With that knowledge, he often wondered how many others were pretending too. The advice was to picture everyone naked, but he was scared he would leer. Richard knew of one way he could get involved in the party, and that was to approach it as a journalist. He would be able to talk and listen if he felt he had a purpose or had the potential to do some good. Self-righteous nonsense really, but it worked for him. The problem was that sometimes he found out things that he'd rather be oblivious to, and the wounds from his last expedition were still open and sensitive. Not to mention the actual wound on his face, which would likely put people off a lengthy chat. All he had to do was look to one of the social media feeds of the people in front of him. There would be a wealth of compliments and love yourself-isms. They had never worked for him, but then again not much had. He searched on his phone for a confidence booster, feeling daft and making sure nobody was close enough to see the screen. The search results returned slowly. He read *if you don't jump you'll never fly*, smiled at his stupidity and stepped closer to the party. It was time to find a story that would help him rewrite his own.

Brad tried not to look at Ava in the way most men do, but it never worked. He supposed that because he had grown up around her that he should see her as more of a... that final word was what he couldn't quite pinpoint. A sister? An aunt? Sometimes he would catch her looking at him with sorrow or regret. Did she feel guilty about the amount of work that his mother took on? Maybe she thought that it had affected his upbringing, just as he did. She was in amongst the crowd now, speaking to the people who had essentially formed a queue to get their chance. Brad watched from the balcony, sipping the champagne and orange juice his mum had given him to toast Ava. He could only taste the bitterness of the orange. Tara was a careful distance from Ava, no more no less. She was ready to swoop in should a conversation go on too long or take an unexpected turn. When someone took a photo of Ava, she would casually ask to see it – usually approving it but fully ready to ask them to delete it if the light was unflattering. That was rarely the case. He knew that Ava was an expert in looking and acting how she was supposed to in almost any situation. He also knew that she had things she was hiding, and secrets that only Tara knew. There would be serious and sombre conversations that he would catch through creaks of doors or ends of phone calls. That was another source of angst – his mother kept things from him that she shared with *her*.

He looked out to the party once more. Nobody looked back. What did Brad have to do to get just a small bit of the attention that was layered on to everyone else? Tara was talking to a man who he didn't recognise now. He swallowed the jealousy with the help of the weak cocktail, but it sat in his stomach like a poison. Even his father hadn't seen him worthy of any attention. Not even an introduction. Brad wondered if he could be one of the men standing below. His mind wandered to a fairytale where he bonded with the man and he taught him all there was to being a man. He could open up to him, move away with him even. It was unlikely, but even the pursuit would make him happy. He put the glass down and decided to attend the party after all. If his mum continued to hide it from him, he knew someone else who might know... *She* knew everything. What was that quote on the front of her notepad again? *When you have a dream, grab it and never let go.*

13

Debauchery it was. There was a slight sense of danger being miles away from the mainland, and it turned out that danger made for a good party starter. All social boundaries had fallen and everybody mixed with one another, sharing drinks and shouting to be heard over the music. Every song, it turned out, was everyone's favourite. The DJ could've played the national anthem of Kazakhstan and at least five people would shriek on their way to the makeshift dance floor. Spotlights shot into the night sky. It was crowded with more stars than the island below it.

Amongst those having the most fun was Richard. He was taking a brief break from being a social butterfly to change his shirt for the third time in his tent. This time, it had been his own drink he spilled. He laughed to himself as he noticed he was back to the original from the morning, the one with the blood from his eye. The memory of the can hitting his face had brought back the pain with it. Why did he turn around when they called him? Maybe he had wanted to be hurt. Sounds outside of his tent. A conversation.

"So what do you say?" Richard knew it as David's voice.

"I don't know why I'm giving you the time of day." The second voice was Hayley's – he knew because she had done some voice-over work for a lingerie brand recently.

"Listen, it was out of my hands before." David spoke as you imagined a showbiz manager would – extremely sure of himself.

"And what would be in it for me this time? I'm not one to accept second place."

"It wouldn't be like that." David assured her.

Richard held his breath in his tent as Hayley pondered her reply. He wasn't sure why, but he felt like his sudden presence wouldn't be welcome.

"I want to know why. Why now?" She said, still maintaining the upper hand.

"Let me get you a drink." David said. They moved away from Richard's tent and he waited a minute before making his way out of the flap.

He took in the scene, deciding on which way to walk knowing fine well that the wrong choice could force him into a deep conversation with someone he had no desire to get to know. David and Hayley had continued their conversation. They were propping up one of the bars. Bradley hung on the periphery of a conversation between young models. He laughed when they laughed and drank when they drank. He emptied a beer and took another from a passing waiter, seemingly on his way to getting drunk. That would be a scalding that Richard would like to eavesdrop on in the morning. Tonight though, it looked like he would get away with it. His mother was dancing like a wild woman as close to the DJ decks as she could get. By the encouragement from the people around her, it appeared that she wasn't known to let loose very often. Good for her, Richard thought. He had been keeping an eye on Ava throughout the night as she made her way through the scores of people who wanted a few minutes with her. Like a bride at a wedding, she was having the least fun. The latest to take her to one side was Herbert, who was talking to her at length. She didn't look in the mood for reminiscing. Her eyes caught Richard's for a second. Before he could point and laugh at her being stuck with him, Herbert followed her gaze and looked over at him too. Richard waved politely, but it wasn't returned. Bobby Taggart had his usual groupies around him. He was being selective with what he offered to the conversation, but each time he did get involved it was met with praise. One had to wonder how all of that false worship affected his judgement.

"Have you left your patch at all?" De Rossi sidled up to him.

"Have you stopped working at all?" He asked in return. De Rossi held his hands up to admit that he hadn't.

"Don't tell me you're not intrigued by these lot a bit?"

"Maybe a bit." Richard conceded.

"Any chance of telling me what interests you? You being the *proper* journalist and all." De Rossi asked with a sarcastic tone. Richard knew he was actually looking for an answer, though.

"No, no chance. You?" Richard replied.

"Wouldn't mind finding out a bit more about this feud between Ava and Hayley – that's what the people want."

"Is it? Or is it what they're used to?"

"Same thing." De Rossi said, handing him the second glass of wine. "Lighten up, Dickson." Richard accepted it and took a swig. Just as he was beginning to relax around his colleague, De Rossi sprung what he had been clearly planning since he saw Richard arrive.

"I've been thinking – about that scandal you're involved in. Good time to get people back on your side." De Rossi said. Richard was sure he knew what was coming, but he wanted to hear it.

"Yeah?" He replied, asking for more.

"Maybe time to tell your story. You know – what happened to your sister."

It wasn't the first time fellow journalists had probed about the potential. He was thankful that nobody had included it in his description when discussing the Young story recently, and he couldn't argue that a bit of sympathy would be welcome just now. Still, to Richard it would be exploiting the memory of Mary, and he couldn't live with that. Surprisingly, he felt calm.

"I'll pass. Although if I ever decide otherwise I'm sure you – the master of boob jobs and affairs – would do a good job." Richard said.

De Rossi laughed at this, clearly comfortable with himself and how he made his money.

"Suit yourself." He said "Let's see where your righteous silence gets you."

They both sipped their drinks for a second before going separate ways. De Rossi towards the bar and Richard to find a drinking companion who didn't know about his past trauma.

The party raged on. Games and music from the DJ were interrupted sporadically with toasts to Ava, each one more flattering than the last. She had smiled politely for most of them, but was deep in a heated conversation with Hayley now on a pair of bean bag chairs away from the main crowd. Tara had continued to drink and, because of that, dance – letting out years of tension in the space of a few hours, probably aware that the next chance she'd get would be a long time away. Brad seemed to be following his mother's lead, now entertaining Paul De Rossi and others who encouraged his rambling observations. Richard, having finally drank enough to drown his social anxiety, was amongst the main crowd, almost dancing and occasionally smiling. Bobby Taggart was one of the people around him. Although they hadn't spoken, he had sent over a drink to Richard who accepted it as a truce for the weekend. Mutterings of Ava's plan for the next day framed the conversations, and some sort of announcement was widely regarded as definitely happening. Richard knew deep down that he was a part of a plan rather than simply a guest. He pushed it out of his head for the night and drank some more. Tomorrow seemed far away. As the music continued and the outdoor heaters glowed red, there was no sign of the fun stopping any time soon...

Richard stepped into the toilets that had been constructed that morning. The light was harsh enough that he knew to avoid looking in the mirror, even in his drunken state. After a few drinks, celebrities had as little respect for public restrooms as the general public did. Urine, wet tissues and even some blood patterned the hard floor. Nosebleeds, he guessed. He had been offered cocaine that evening about as many times as he had been told someone's name, always declining to cling onto whatever self-control he had left. Drugs had never agreed with his rapidly anxious mind, and now was probably the worst point in his life to test that. He slumped backwards in the cubicle and the door caught him. As he relieved himself, he was missing more of the toilet than he hit. No point in cleaning up now – it would be like taking a shot glass to an oil spill. It made it easier that he wasn't the first to make the mess. Gang mentality, he thought – *someone else will do it.* As he began to think of pissing on the seat in public toilets as a wider metaphor for society, his heavy eyelids started to shut. Someone crashed into the cabin, waking him. He flushed the toilet with his foot and left the cubicle.

"I tried that earlier." He said to David, who was washing his face in the comically small sink. "Doesn't work does it?"

David just smiled a fake smile at him in the mirror and went to get some tissues to dry himself off, so Richard left. He could be sure that he had heard him say something, but in this state it took a lot for him to manoeuvre his body to turn around. He kept going towards the crowd. A woman stopped him in his tracks, catching him as he took an age to stop moving forwards.

"I had no idea about you." She said, handing him a whisky. What was going on here? Best to just play along, he thought. Had he met her? The voice was familiar but his vision was clouded and the strobe light didn't illuminate her for long enough.

"I'm a man of many surprises." He said, taking a sip and enjoying the burn, although it was less noticeable once you got into double figures.

"You seemed so... normal." She said. Her high-pitched voice didn't sound nice when she had to shout. It made Richard want to scratch his eardrum.

"I'm anything but normal." He said, leaning close to her ear. It was more from the alcohol than anything else, but she did the same, her shoulder close to his chest.

"Can we dance?" She asked, slowing her words.

"We can try." He said, sloshing some whisky in the direction of the music. He tried to glance at his watch, but needed to stare to take the information in. 11:45. He had time before meeting Ava. All the booze in the world wouldn't make him forget about her.

DAY 2

14

A hangover and a helicopter overhead made for quite a painful awakening. Richard saw a smooth leg slip out of his tent before the person it was attached to struggled with the zip to close the flap.

"Just leave it." He snapped – angry at the cruelties of the world, but more at himself for making it worse. Who just left him? And how did they end up here? How much damage control was due and how many people did it involve? He hadn't had to piece together a night like this for some time. Oh well, his stock in the world couldn't plummet much further – time to own it. He sat up slowly, getting his bearings and reminding himself not to test his balance close to the cliffs today. People were rushing around – what time was it? Too early. He knew deep down that they would be going straight past his tent to reach something or someone more important, but the alcohol induced anxiety tricked him into thinking people were coming for him. He stayed silent as the silhouettes got smaller on the burnt orange plastic sheets surrounding him. Was that a scream? Yes, definitely a scream. More than one. Collective terror.

Her face was a mixture of swelling purples, reds and whites. Her blue eyes could almost be found amongst it all, although they seemed closer to grey now. Grains of sand had found their way into every little wound and dent, and there were plenty of them. More than any person could survive. On her descent, her leg along with her dress had caught one of the sharp rocks and been ripped to shreds. Any blood that could find its way out of her twisted and mangled frame had done so and made its way towards the ocean. Ava Hart was dead, and so were her secrets. The island seemed sinister now, despite the sun still shining as it did the day before. There was poison in the breeze, and the shadows from the cliffs were darker.

"Flying your pals in from all over the world to witness your suicide? That's a new kind of sad." The local cop, Murphy, had a poetic accent only found on the very edges of Scotland. Not being accustomed to finding many dead bodies, he held his hat on his chest as his colleagues did their work, exposing a bald patch that was conquering his hair convincingly. A scene of the crime officer looked away from her camera to shake her head. She pointed at a single wound on the back of Ava's scalp – the rest were on her front where she had collided with the jagged rocks and ultimately hit the ground.

"A lethal blow?" Murphy asked.

"Looks like it sir. They'll be able to tell us more when she's flown to the mainland, but I'd bet on murder." She lifted the camera and found more angles to capture, determined to not give the big city force anything to moan about when they inevitably turned up.

Chief Inspector Murphy lifted his head and squinted at the crowd forming atop the cliff. The sun reduced the individuals to shadows. One of them could be a killer.

Richard heard the news as he moved through the crowd, but he chose not to believe it straightaway. It was a joke – Ava's wicked sense of humour showing itself in a cruel way. Totally misjudged, but they would laugh about it together later. They would be together again. He would apologise for not meeting her when she asked him to last night. He got caught up with the mystery woman – she would understand. He could picture Ava's reaction now, a quiet kissing of her teeth and a roll of the eyes before a smile that let him know it was all going to be okay. Their friendship had survived worse. He avoided the edge of the cliff where the crowd was and made for the trail down to the beach. Ignoring the glaring signs that this wasn't a prank. Stumbling his way onto the beach, the white suits sweeping the area shot all of the naïve notions out of his head for good.

"Sir, you can't be here." A female voice, although he didn't know who it came from. Upon seeing Ava he dropped to the ground, knees smashing off the smooth rocks in amongst the sand. The police officers around him allowed the mourning for a few seconds before approaching him.

"Sir, are you a family member?"
Richard shook his head, opening his mouth and preparing words that never came. He didn't know where Ava's family were. Probably in the house she grew up in on the outskirts of Glasgow, not understanding the extent of their daughter's fame other than knowing it was enough to pay off their mortgage and organise trips around the world. Certainly, they would be safe in the knowledge that her lifestyle wasn't one that would lead to an early grave. Their phone would be ringing soon – her mum taking a break from cooking to answer it, clueless that her heart was about to be broken beyond repair. A male officer was helping Richard to his feet with big hands under each arm. Firm enough to show authority, but still managing to be considerate.

"Up you get, son, you're only hurting yourself." Chief Inspector Murphy took Richard to the side and sat him down on a mound of long grass. "Get your breath." His hand remained on Richard's shoulder as Tara and Brad stumbled onto the beach much like he had. David followed right behind them. They made it closer to the body than Richard did, and so were stopped with more force while being informed it was a crime scene. Tara was whimpering like a hurt dog as she clung onto Brad with the strength that only a mother can conjure. David simply stared at Ava's body, willing her to surprise them all one last time. To beat the odds against her like she had all her life. The scene of the crime officers moved in again. For the final time, a camera flashed on Ava Hart.

15

The mood was a strange one. Richard got the feeling that half of the guests were as excited as the others were traumatised. The influencers and social media stars among them were certainly thinking of the most respectful way to capitalise on the tragedy. Word hadn't seemed to have gotten out just yet, but De Rossi was making calls like he was an old woman at the stroke of midnight on Hogmanay.

Two detectives from Glasgow, Rankin and Donnelly, had arrived on the island like stars of a BBC drama. They had swiftly informed the guests that they were locking the place down until the case of Ava's death was closed. There was chatter amongst the group about whether or not they were allowed to do such a thing, but nobody had the guts or knowledge to speak out. Image was everything here, and everyone was acutely aware that a protest at staying on the island may make them look inconsiderate, or even suspicious. Hell, they were booked here for another couple of days – did any of them really have an excuse to leave?

As the two detectives began their initial enquiries, their colleagues took over a marquee that was previously a bar area. This was to be their island HQ for the foreseeable. Another small team of officers searched the house that Ava had been staying in. To Richard, it didn't look like they suspected suicide. He was finding it hard to accept that himself. He had started a bit of research into any major changes in her life recently. Changes that she would have probably informed him of if he had kept his word and met her the night before. He had managed to wrestle his mind away from the guilt associated with this, and the questions of if it would've made a difference had he showed up. The guilt would come though, it was only a matter of time.

In terms of life events that could have triggered suicide, he found none. She had recently given up the majority shareholder position of her main business and brand, which had comfortably set her up for life. A reason to celebrate, if anything. Her love life had miraculously remained out of the press for most of her career, but even so Richard had gathered that she was happily single. She had feuds, like any 21st century celebrity, but nothing he could find was serious enough to dent her confidence, never mind cause depression. Wasn't that the cruel thing about depression though? If everyone could spot it as it was happening, then it wouldn't lead to so many deaths.

The grass he was sitting on was still wet from the morning dew and it was soaking through his shorts. The hangover that had seemed like the worst of his problems had been replaced by a deep sadness as he watched the helicopter take Ava's body from the island and on its way to the morgue. Her parents would have been informed now. He contemplated phoning his own. His Dad had phoned twice when the sexual assault story scandal had made its way offline and reached old media. He hadn't answered, only deepening the gulf between them that had made itself known when his Mum died years earlier. She hadn't told anyone about the cancer or how aggressive it was until she had to enter palliative care. Richard couldn't understand it at the time, but as he grew older he started to understand why she had made that decision. Had Ava done the same? Did she come to this island to end her life? DI Rankin was about to answer that for him – he had gathered the guests in front of the house.

"As we stand, we're treating Ava Hart's death as suspicious. Now that has a few consequences for you all." He removed his jacket, revealing some sweat patches on his grey shirt. He looked the type to play bad cop rather than good, and didn't hide his disdain for the entitled people hanging on his every word. Richard placed him as mid 40s, although his general demeanor was someone who was counting the days until retirement. The salt and pepper crew cut he sported was army-esque – he either served or wanted to emulate the authority and discipline of someone who had.

"First, you'll all be questioned. Trust me, I'm going to enjoy it as little as you are. Second, this is now a crime scene and a major investigation. If I finally find some fucking signal around here, the last thing I want to see is your detailed theories on YouTube. No information leaves this island before it comes through me or my colleague here."

DS Donnelly was standing cross armed next to her superior. Her eyes, wrinkled and almost closed, were scanning the crowd for any traces of disobedience. A good detective act – she knew nobody would likely be giving anything away just now, but her stare may panic them into doing so.

"Third." DI Rankin spoke up again, ending any chatter. "I have little reason to believe that Miss Hart's death was suicide." He paused for effect here, and the mouths of those who hadn't considered anything else hit the floor. "Now an accident isn't out of the question, but neither is murder." There were gasps. Richard, watching from the back, wondered what the detective was gaining from laying all of his cards out on the table like this. Was he hoping for a blame game? He supposed there was nothing to lose, and now absolutely nobody would consider leaving the island.

"You'll be informed when we would like to speak to you. In the meantime, make yourself comfortable, and get your tents back up." Rankin finished his address and entered the island's house again, with Donnelly following after another glare. Inside, she gave up the act and wanted to know the game plan.

"Do you really think murder, sir?" Her voice was high-pitched and caring, the polar opposite of Rankin's gruff, authoritative tone.

"Most likely a drunken accident, but someone out there knows more than they've offered so far. Figure they'll be willing to admit seeing her stumble or play fighting with her if they think the alternative is being labelled a killer." Donnelly nodded as if she had understood all along. "Get me a background on everyone out there. Prioritise those closest to her and anyone with a record." Rankin continued. "Let's get off this fucking island as soon as we can."

"Not a big fan of the rich and famous, sir?" Donnelly quipped.

"Famous? I've never seen any of those idiots in my life."

Bobby Taggart seemed relaxed, almost content. Even if he had been involved, the family's lawyers would make sure nothing came of it. It was this bulletproof lifestyle that gave him the arrogance that was almost expected of him. Some had it easy, others had it tough – he would be serving nobody if he switched to the less appealing side. Why apologise for the wealth he was born into? That wasn't the Taggart way – they were deserving of everything that came to them. His father had disapproved of Bobby's courting of the celebrity lifestyle. The old man didn't understand that this was where money went nowadays, not the country club. Middle Eastern Sheiks, Russian oligarchs, Asian business giants – they all wanted to be seen with superstars, and they had the money to make it happen. Bobby had spoken to the manager of the events company and had offered to pay them to continue to serve the guests – they weren't going anywhere anyway, he had pointed out. The cappuccino he was holding was worth every penny. He let the steam warm his face as he scanned the crowd looking for Richard Dickson. He found him, alone and in the shade beside the house. It was time to toy with him.

"I don't believe we've met officially." Bobby said, not bothering to extend a hand.

"I was hoping it would stay that way." Richard replied, leaning against a quad bike.

"Now, now." Bobby warned him, looking for a place to lay his empty mug as if for his whole life it had been someone's job to make sure he was never without a side table. He settled for the grass.

"Listen, Taggart. You don't like me because of the story about your friend, I get it. Ever think it could be true?" Richard saw no need to be pleasant.

"I've no doubt that it could be true. Shall we take a ride?" Bobby kicked one of the wheels of a quad bike with his polished brogue. "They said don't leave the island, so we won't be breaking the rules."

Richard doubted that Bobby Taggart had ever worried about breaking the rules.

Brad stepped away from the window as the two men started the quad bikes. They weren't pretending to grieve like he had to. He had watched them closely – how they were acting in the aftermath, if they would still laugh and joke and do what people did. He had never dealt with death before, and it was confusing him. He couldn't shake a feeling of optimism that his life would now have less restraint. He had certainly wished her away plenty of times before, hoping that his mother would have more time for him and a normal life. It had crossed his mind that deep down maybe she would be happy, but every time she saw him she burst into tears once more.

16

Bobby Taggart's jawline, hairline and posture all screamed well bred. Richard had often wondered in general how much of this was upbringing and how much genetics. Either way, he fit his role perfectly.

The island's terrain was accustomed to vehicles like the ones they rode, offering a flat track at almost every turn. The noise of the quadbikes was allowing Richard some time to think about what he was doing, and if it mattered. He knew Bobby was close to Gareth Young, or close enough to contribute to his political career. Maybe it was only the man's career he was interested in – if Young became too hot to handle he could just back another horse. Still, why entertain Richard at all? And what was his relationship with Ava? They pulled up at the old lighthouse, its frame towering menacingly above them. Bobby turned off the engine and watched Richard as he did the same.

"Shame, old buildings like this. They still have their uses, you know." Bobby strode towards the disused lighthouse, expecting as he always did for the door to be open for him. Richard recognised his clumsy attempts at symbolism, probably born from an education memorizing Shakespeare paired with a lack of imagination.

"You'd be happy to see it knocked down I assume?" Bobby posed the question as he slid the heavy latch to unlock the door.

"No, it's a part of history – why remove any trace of it?" Richard replied as he entered the building, hearing his last few words form an echo. The spherical shape of the room induced dizziness in him. Solid white bricks were hosting a battle between orange rust and green moss, and three clunky radiators looked a kick away from toppling. Shelves remained but their contents had long gone – taken as souvenirs or blown and disintegrated by the elements. Richard's interest in the place peaked, so much so that he forgot who he was sharing the space with. Bobby was ascending a concrete staircase that made half a spiral up the wall. Richard followed.

"I read your *article*." Bobby said, emphasizing the word to make it sound like a child's game.

"I'd love to hear your thoughts – you're just my target audience." Richard replied, joining Bobby on the first floor. This was the living quarters, as shown by the single steel bed frame beside a circular window missing any traces of glass or cover. The wind whipped through and blew dust making the air heavy and breaths uncomfortable.

"I thought it was careless, but it's what I've come to expect from small pond dwellers." Richard had been called worse, so let it go without comment.

"How so?" He asked. They were still busying themselves with the task of exploring.

"These exposés you write might change things for a brief moment in time, or for a small group of people, but more important change is going on. Yes, what you reveal is important to some, but a tiny piece of the bigger puzzle. For you to have your way would be like a pebble derailing a freight train."

"You don't think people have the right to know who they're voting for?" Richard asked.

"People, largely, shouldn't be overwhelmed with too much information. It doesn't lend itself to progress."

"And what progress is that? Certainly not the treatment of women."

"Gareth Young is a doer, much like many people on this island. Your small victory may change one life, but you'd be cashing out before seeing how many more could be changed if he was allowed to progress. A drop in the ocean." As he finished speaking, Bobby flicked a piece of metal from the window and sent it to the water below them.

"You won't be shocked to hear that we view the world very differently, Bobby." Richard said, looking up and deciding whether or not to climb the steel ladders to the top.

"Yes, agreed." Bobby said. "Which brings me on to why you're here. I can't help but be curious..." Bobby had made the decision for them, putting a polished shoe on the first rusty rung. "Or is it a question of who you're here for?" He shouted back, disappearing into the hatch above. Richard knew there must be things that Bobby Taggart would like to keep private – had his very presence rattled him? Maybe the Young story did work. Hadn't that been his righteous goal as a young journalist – to have the respect of the people whom he felt the world should know more about?

"It's purely personal. Ava is – was – an old friend." Richard said. On his first grasp of the ladder, splinters of rust penetrated his skin. Another ailment to add to the list as his body started to feel like his mental state personified. He reached the top level and marveled at the views out to the ocean. The windows were grimy, but the pure unfiltered brightness of the landscape still made its way through clearly. The mechanism that took the centre of the room and reached the ceiling was vast – more cogs and wheels than electronics.

"I find that hard to believe, considering the lifestyles of some of our cohabitants." Bobby enunciated with perfection.

"You don't think she killed herself?"

"I've made it 30 years without helping the press – now seems like a strange time to start."

"Apart from there's a young woman dead?" Richard locked his eyes on Bobby's now, searching for a drop of humanity.

"And plenty here who will be relieved." Bobby offered, raising an eyebrow to tell Richard that he would go no further.

"Spit it out, Taggart." Richard said, surprising himself more than Bobby who simply smiled.

"Suicide – people treat it in such a black and white manner, don't they?"

"How so?"

"Well, if you put a gun to your head or jump off a bridge, it's suicide. The physical act of killing yourself. But what about making a series of decisions that lead you to getting killed – is it not the same?"

"It depends on your intentions. Putting yourself in danger is different from trying to get yourself killed. Soldiers dying at war aren't committing suicide." Richard replied.

"Ah, but are they not? They chose to go knowing the risks, didn't they?" Bobby asked.

"What is it you know?"

"Too many people want me to know things, Richard – it's impossible to keep it all to memory."

"I'm sure the detectives will be satisfied." Richard said. Bobby Taggart chuckled at the idea of law and order. "So no suicide?"

"As I said, that depends on your definition."
Richard, as much as he didn't want to, considered what the socialite had to say.

"Maybe that will focus your attention on something more important, and your current scandal can be forgotten." Bobby said. He moved out of the way of the viewing window, exposing Richard to the emptiness outside. Empty, but alive with currents and waves. Richard was beginning to think that there was a story to be found on this island after all, and maybe it was the reason for his invite.

Ava's death had reached the masses. De Rossi has been careful to warn his editor to leave his name off of the initial story, something that would have pained him to do. Still, despite his efforts, it didn't fool DI Rankin.

"Paul De Rossi. You Italian?" Rankin sat down across from the journalist at his makeshift desk, previously the house's dining room table.

"It's in the blood. My father's grandfather was -"

"So no then." Rankin cut him off, already losing what little patience he had brought with him to the island. "You must think you've struck gold here." He continued.

"How so?" De Rossi had been badgering the police for years

and was well aware that the two professions needed one another more than ever. There were plenty of people on the island who would be phased by their presence, but he wasn't one.

"Story of the year isn't it? A mysterious death of someone who was at the top of her game. Peak of her career." Rankin rolled his r's and spoke every word from the throat.

"Peak? I'm not so sure. There were whispers that she was about to make a grand exit." De Rossi said. Rankin raised his hand, reminding him that they were dealing with death here and his innuendos wouldn't be tolerated. The journalist conceded with a shrug.

"Is that what you heard?" The detective asked.

"Something to the extent of finally moving her life out of the spotlight after almost 20 years. Could be bullshit again."

"Again?" Rankin glanced up from his notes.

"She took a year or so break at the start of her fame. Only came back bigger. I always reckoned it was strategic." Paul De Rossi had risen through the ranks of his profession as Ava had hers, writing stories about her along the way. Over the years circulation had dropped, colleagues made redundant and printers closed, but the demand for details of a celebrity's personal life hadn't faltered. He told others that his coverage was key to her star power and thought that the invite to this weekend had proven as much.

"You have any reason to suspect something a bit more sinister going on here?" Rankin posed the question with calmness, but it was easy to see that he begrudged having to ask the tabloids to point him in the right direction. Still, a result was a result and there would be plenty of eyes on this. If the findings from the lab said as he predicted, suicide wouldn't stand up to the scrutiny.

"Listen, I know this world is new to you and seems tame compared to the gang feuds and people traffickers you're used to, but those people out there can be every bit as vindictive." De Rossi said.

"I find that hard to believe. Think any of them is capable of murder?" Rankin asked, squeezing a pen underneath the table to let out some tension.

"Now that would be story of the year. But murder? No. As much as I'd enjoy seeing you sweat, and what it would mean for my web clicks, I can't see it."

"And why invite a killer to your birthday party?"

"Exactly." De Rossi nodded his head, but stopped mid motion. "Although one thing did strike me as odd."

The Detective Inspector raised an eyebrow to encourage him to continue.

"The guest list is like a who's who of her career. People she hadn't dealt with in months, sometimes years. And she certainly didn't get on with a lot of them. It didn't feel like a party when I arrived – more like a set up."

"As much as it pains me to say this, you might be more useful than I thought." Rankin scribbled something down before continuing. "Sit down with DS Donnelly and take her through anyone you were surprised to see on the list, will you?" It was a request, but not really.

"And the story is mine when you figure it all out?" De Rossi asked. The Detective didn't respond, but the unspoken agreement was enough.

De Rossi left the room in search of DS Donnelly. Rankin knew fine well from experience that circumstances created most killings, not the people involved. Push someone far enough and that made them capable, even if they weren't the day before. Yes, everything was about circumstances, but he could see none here to awaken a killer. Despite the gossip he had just been offered, he couldn't make the connection to murder, and he wasn't known to be someone who ruled things out without careful thought. His phone rang as he was close to convincing himself that there was no foul play.

"DI Rankin." He answered, knowing that the conversation coming would dictate that coming days and how hard they would be for him. The voice on the other end of the line confirmed signs of strangulation, a struggle and a fatal blow to the head. Ava Hart had been dead before plummeting to the beach below.

17

Whispers from the interview room started to make their way throughout the group of people on the island – there was a murderer in their midst. Nervous giggles and even the odd tasteless joke didn't do anything to curb the sense of dread. What had been a camaraderie driven drama was now a suspicious standoff. Each guest ran through how likely they were to be suspected and every one of them, through paranoia or otherwise, came up with at least one reason to think that they could be. Any drunken friendships that had been made the night before were sent straight back to stranger status. If you had arrived alone, you were to remain that way. Of course, each one of them had their hunches, and it would take only the slightest of tensions for them all to turn to mob mentality. DI Rankin, DS Donnelly and their colleagues now had a new problem to deal with as a matter of urgency – was there a chance that their killer would strike again?

Richard was in his tent, listening to the worried conversations outside. He couldn't quite grasp anything of substance from them. He was channeling his guilt into an investigation – determined to find out more about Ava and what could possibly lead to someone benefiting from murdering her. What was it she had said to him? *I want you to tell my story.* At the time he had thought nothing of it. An empty promise to pen a biography in ten years when she was leaving show business behind. She was just being nice, telling him in a roundabout way that his career would pick up again. Now, it seemed that he had missed the hidden message behind it. Ava wanted to expose something, reveal something she knew that wouldn't go down well with certain people. But who? Find that person and find the killer, he thought. From the limited information the police were giving away, it seemed calculated and not a crime of passion. Did that meant that someone had arrived on the island the day before knowing what they were going to do? He thought back to the welcome gathering and the evening party – was there someone who was acting strange? Or someone who was making sure that they didn't do anything strange at all? Memories of murder mystery nights in his parents' house came to the front of his mind. Neighbours and old friends would spend weeks preparing their costumes before the event, practicing accents that would always turn out shockingly bad. The game always descended into a farce after a number of bottles of wine had been opened. Once or twice they had ended up in physical fights. His parents had put a ban on them after the butcher punched the butler for staring at the lady of the manor's chest. Richard remembered crouching at the top of the stairs to listen to the shouting matches between characters, real life spilling into the act. Sometimes he would read the revealing card to find out who the murderer was before anyone arrived at the house. He'd listen in and watch from afar how the person played the game – some would try to blend into the background, but most made themselves the centre of attention.

Frustrated with the speed of his internet booster, he fired an email to an old friend asking her to send any pictures she had from the final year of high school. If he was going to delve into Ava's fame, he may as well start at the beginning. As he waited on a response, he started going back into the archives of news coverage. Online stories hadn't been as constant in the early 2000s, but the important stuff still made it to the internet, and Ava was clearly important. The real, consistent coverage started upon her return to the public eye after a year or two out of the spotlight – the period of time that Richard hadn't reached out. Maybe if he had back then he would understand more about her. The truth was, he had always wanted to, but was scared of looking like he cared only because she was famous. When she burst back onto the scene, the first few months of coverage was a search for information about her disappearance. She gave little comment, giving out cute lines like *"I'm here now, isn't that all that matters?"* and *"if I told you, you wouldn't believe me."* The concluding story on the saga, written by up and comer Paul De Rossi, called the whole thing a shrewd PR move that had paid off. Richard, as much as it pained him, was inclined to agree. Such was Ava's fame from then on that only a handful of the stories actually involved her. The majority was speculation and rumour, always either confirmed or denied by *"those close to her"* or *"someone in her inner circle."* Tara, Richard thought. If there was anybody who was close to knowing Ava's secrets, it would be her friend and assistant of 18 years. Richard searched her name and little else of note came up on the screen – almost as if she didn't have a life of her own. She was Ava's shadow. There was one interesting piece written a few years back from a corporate magazine, its target audience PAs and office managers. It was headlined *The woman beside the most powerful woman in the world.* Tara had given a more candid interview than was expected of her, covering the joys and pitfalls of working in such a high-pressure environment. Why was it worth it? Because Ava was a friend. In fact, that's how it all began. Tara, a few years older than her future boss, had left school dreaming of a career in broadcasting. On Ava's first day on set of the children's TV show she was presenting, Tara had been given the task of simply keeping her company. *"I knew the way things worked to an extent, and I think the producers thought I would be a calming influence. We were similar in age and we hit it off immediately. Since then, well she hasn't been able to live without me."* Tara had told the reporter. Richard wondered just how close the two women had become over the years, and knew there was only one person now that he could ask.

He left the tent and shivered as huge clouds moved in front of the sun. It felt like days had passed since Ava's body was discovered on the beach, but in reality it had only been a matter of hours. The initial police activity had died down, sweeps and searches made, and most were now just involved in the admin of organising interviews with each of the guests. Some people were catching up on the sleep stolen from them from the rude awakening that morning, others were sheepishly chatting together or on the phone. Even the small amount of activity made Richard's head ache again. He cursed himself for drinking that much the night before, although couldn't remember at what point things had gotten bad. He had been indulging in a bit of self destruction, that much was clear, but enough to not remember a thing? He made a note to rack his brains and retrace his steps if need be, if only so he had something to offer the police when the time came for his interview.

He made it into the house with little fuss, the officers in charge of guarding the door seemingly searching for a reason to ask him to remain outside but coming up with nothing. The stairs creaked as he made his way upstairs. He took pause at the top and looked into the master bedroom. Tara was sitting on the edge of the bed, unaware that she was being watched. She held her stomach and stared blankly ahead of her, not crying now but the evidence was there. Any flushes of colour Richard had noticed when he met her had left, leaving her looking pale and lifeless. He cleared his throat as he entered, hoping to avoid startling her.

"How are you keeping?" He said, falling into the trap of such an obvious question. He took a seat by the window.

"Oh, you know. Terrible." It was clear Tara had said the same thing to a lot of others already today. Her mind was elsewhere, trying to summon every last bit of organizational skill she had built over the years to help her comprehend what had happened and what came next.

"I'm trying to work it all out in my head and it's a nightmare. I can only imagine what it's like for you." She nodded a thank you. Richard knew he was going to have to do most of the talking. "Is Brad okay?" He continued. Her eyes met his. And then darted across the hall to a closed door.

"Brad? He's fine, why wouldn't he be? He's fine isn't he?"

"Sorry, I didn't mean to worry you. I just meant, was he coping with it all okay?" As Richard spoke, her heart stopped racing.

"I'm not really sure. They were so close. Closer than we were sometimes." Tara placed a delicate pinky on her eye and wiped the lid. Richard was left wondering if she meant closer than her and Ava, or closer than her and her son. He decided not to push it.

"Did she seem okay to you? You know, before." He asked.
Tara appeared to be studying him, seeing how much she trusted him. She cast her mind back to Ava assuring him that she could the day before, and she wanted to do nothing but honour her memory and wishes from now on.

"Honestly, Richard – I wish I could tell you. I don't know what came over me, but from about 10 o'clock onwards I can't remember a thing. Never in my life have I got myself in that state. Never. My head, my stomach, my body – I feel like I've been hit by a bus and then reversed over for good measure. I read a bit into drink spiking – I know you shouldn't self diagnose, but -" As if on cue, Tara's throat spasmed and her hand instinctively shot to her mouth. She made it to the bathroom in three strides, leaving the door open. As Richard listened to the hacking sounds of her vomiting, he felt his own stomach gurgle and his own head pound. His muscles ached too. His gag reflex had been tested a few times during the morning. He had put it down to shame and distress, but now it was clear to him that whatever Tara had, so did he.

18

DI Rankin looked at the sheets of paper in front of him and began to taste defeat for the first time in his career. Never before had he had such little inclination about a suspect. Sure, he'd been wrong in the past, way off the mark even, but at least that set off a chain of thought that led to him being right. Right now, the picture he could paint was abstract, and he absolutely hated abstract paintings. He had a dislike for anything that wasn't practical – this island included. He longed for the claustrophobic streets of Glasgow where the buildings stopped nature from making his eyes itch and his nose burn. Most of all, he hated the people here. Never had he seen such collective arrogance and entitlement. Every question and answer given to him in each interview screamed self-service. The only good thing was he had them all in one place, but he had to work quickly before flights were booked to every corner of the world. The pressure was on to get a result before people started arguing their rights to leave the island. The truth was that any of them could leave if they wanted to, but they knew that the finger of guilt would point right at them. He had three interviews left to conduct, and although he held little hope for an admission, he was particularly interested in each of them. Tara, Ava Hart's longtime assistant and friend. If anyone knew any grimy details it would be her. Richard Dickson, a journalist already embroiled in his own scandal. Rankin had been informed that Ava was supposed to meet him on the night of her death. Third was Bradley, Tara's son. A weird kid who had been carted around the world because of his mother's vocation. He wouldn't be surprised if he could find some sort of resentment towards Ava within the young man.

Other than that, there were stacks of paper dedicated to celebrity feuds and fall outs that Miss Hart had been a part of. They read like Greek to DI Rankin, who inwardly admitted that his two daughters were probably more qualified than he was to solve this case. He hoped that the lab would offer something stronger – calling them was a last ditch and embarrassing option, but an option nonetheless.

DS Donnelly watched her mentor slumped at the desk, frustration coming out of his pores. It was like watching a vegan trying to work out the best way to carve a chicken. Being the younger officer by 6 years, she was a bit more familiar with the people on the island than he was. She often cursed herself for scrolling through social media feeds and gossip sites with a gin in hand, knowing fine well there was a perfectly good gym at HQ. Still, she was in better shape than any of her male colleagues, so she had some leeway. She had seen too many women in the field bow down to the pressures imposed by a mostly male environment. Many PCs she knew had forced themselves into an interest in the football, seeing it as a way to bond and progress. Bullshit. As far as DS Donnelly was concerned, the less testosterone and egos present in policing the better. She took a break from the transcripts she was pouring over and stepped outside, immediately sensing nerves and hostility from the party guests. The thick heels on her shoes struggled with the terrain as she made her way down to the beach, and she cursed the fact that others' potential judgement, specifically DI Rankin's, stopped her from packing her walking boots. The detective slipped under the tape and approached the area where the body was discovered. They had had to work quickly that morning, being completely at the mercy of the elements. Sure enough, the tide and wind had worked together to almost all indication that a lifeless body ever lay there.

"What were you hiding Ava?" Donnelly whispered as she crouched to touch the sand. She looked out to the ocean, well aware that the reason for Ava's death must have stemmed from across it. Did the killer know she wouldn't be leaving the island? Or had they come to offer a warning and then not liked her response? There was a history of show business types being involved with the shady underworld but, as far as Donnelly knew, today it was just that – a history. She couldn't find a jot of evidence that Ava had owed money to people, or got herself caught up in criminal activity. In fact, Ava appeared to have worked her way to a point of financial freedom, and done so in a way that there weren't many pieces of the pie that had to be shared. The woman had earned her own money by being beautiful, savvy and ruthless. So if not cash, then what? She dug her hands in the sand looking for answers and, to her surprise, came up with one. DS Donnelly pulled out a small, golden badge that had refused to be swept away by the water. In bold, it read **RE-EMPOWER** alongside the symbol for the female gender.

Richard was getting nowhere. Bobby Taggart had said that plenty of people on the island would be relieved that Ava was gone, but he couldn't find a single strand or story to back that up. Still, she clearly had something to spill. He had considered that his hindsight was blurred by the events, but no – he was certain that she had planned to reveal something this weekend. Not just to him, but to the carefully selected guest list as well. She had called it a game, and if Richard hadn't seen the bloodied and bruised body himself, he would probably think it was one.

"Dickson." A shout from outside the tent – he guessed it was his turn to be questioned.

As he followed the uniformed officer towards the house, he wondered if everyone had been subjected to the suspicious glares he was getting.

DI Rankin and DS Donnelly were both seated at the table as he was escorted into the room. The view from the window on the other side offered a landscape untouched by humanity. He sat across from the detectives, holding very little hope that he was going to get an easy time.

"Trouble seems to turn up wherever you do, Mr Dickson." DI Rankin, the male officer, started proceedings. Both sets of eyes were watching Richard's every expression and muscle twitch.

"Wrong place at the right time, I suppose." Richard said, prompting a quick sniff from Rankin.

"When did you last see Ava Hart?" DS Donnelly took over.

"I saw her throughout the night at the party. Last spoke to her before it. She was in high demand."

"And how did your last conversation go?"

Richard had thought of not much else since that morning. How did it go? Ava had been dropping signals that he was too naïve to pick up. Sadly, the time passing had only made them more confusing. The conversation was about him, and she had asked about Jane. Something in his gut told him that he shouldn't be telling the police that.

"It was normal, for our first proper conversation in years."

"Was Miss Hart interested in your recent story about Gareth Young?" Donnelly continued, not giving him a second to think between responses.

"It may have come up briefly."

"In what fashion?" DI Rankin interjected, showing himself to be a man with a short temper that had the potential still to shrink further.

"She had asked if I was coping okay – that sort of thing."

"She wanted to help?" DS Donnelly spoke again now, making Richard think that the double act was more rehearsed than he had originally given them credit for.

"I wouldn't say that. Ava knew there was nothing she could do." Richard said.

"You didn't ask her for help?"

"No."

DI Rankin shifted in his chair and rested both elbows on the table.

"Suppose you did ask for help." He said. "Wouldn't be nice to be turned down, would it?"

"I didn't ask her for help. I'm not in the business of supposing." Richard said, struggling to keep a lid on his impatience.

"Not what I've heard." Rankin muttered.

Richard blinked slowly, seeing where they were going now. He was a suspect. He tensed his legs under the table hoping that he could hide the angst.

"We've heard from a few people that you had arranged to meet Miss Hart later on. Is that true?" DS Donnelly picked it back up again.

Who could've known about that? He asked himself - but was careful not to take too long of a pause. He was answering on pure instinct with only seconds between deciding what to say and what to keep to himself. Silence would be the last option.

"We had talked about it, yeah."

"Here's my problem." DI Rankin said, leaning back again and cracking his knuckles. "I know you're going to tell me that that meeting didn't happen, aren't you? But I've got a dead body here and nobody is admitting to being the last person seeing her alive. Would you blame me for thinking that it could have been you?"

A double question to throw him off – he could implicate himself by answering either. Years of over-analysis of every social situation he'd ever been in, it had turned out, was quite helpful when being interrogated about a murder.

"I was with someone for the night. They'll tell you that it didn't happen." Richard replied. Rankin did better than Donnelly at hiding his surprise, but they were both shook a little.

"And who might that be?" He asked. Now for the tricky part.

"I can't remember." It hung in the air as a smile creeped across DI Rankin's face as if it was going to grow wider than his cheeks.

"Look, I know how this is going to sound, but I've got a feeling my drink was spiked." Richard muttered it, knowing how daft it sounded.

"You have a feeling?" Rankin didn't hide his sarcasm.

"Well if I was sure I wouldn't have drank it, would I?" This was met with a warning look from both detectives. It wouldn't bode well for Richard if he took that tone again. "Some things are coming back to me, but slowly. I'll be able to find whoever I was with."

"Would you be surprised to hear that you're not the first person to tell me that their drink was spiked?"

"Surprise is something I'm finding it difficult to experience just now, Detective." Richard pressed his fingers into the bridge of his nose, forgetting about his swollen eye and recoiling from the sharp pain. "But if more people have said it then doesn't that give you a reason to believe me?"

"It could do, or it could tell me that you were the one doing the spiking." DI Rankin pointed out.

"Do I need a lawyer?" Richard asked, deflated.

"You tell me." Rankin said, pleased that his case just got the steroid injection it had desperately needed.

Curiosity and justice for Ava weren't driving Richard any longer – he had to catch the killer before his life took yet another downward spiral, this time one he wouldn't be able to climb back from. If his stomach had anything in it he was sure he'd vomit.

19

Brad could hear his mother retching from the room next to his. The police were kind enough to let them stay in the house as they occupied the downstairs and scanned Ava's room for any clues as to why she was murdered. He ached for this to all be over, for them to move on together. Maybe she would let him out more often, he could meet some people his own age. If he was popular, he'd get the attention for a change. The vomiting started again, although he doubted that there would be anything left in her stomach to bring up by now. Of course he felt bad about giving her that drink, but how was he to know how bad things would get? Everybody else was allowed to have secrets, so he decided that this would be his.

"Brad?"

He shot round on the bed as if he had been caught doing something he shouldn't be. It was one of the reporters – the one who had been obsessed with Ava. He asked if he could come in. Brad nodded. They had been talking the night before and he seemed okay.

"How are you?" He asked. Brad considered his response, still not quite knowing how he should be acting.

"Tired." He said. Paul De Rossi nodded and perched himself cautiously on a seat close to the bed.

"Must be tough for you." He smiled. "Were you close with her?"

Out of sight, Brad made a fist until his knuckles turned white. They only pretended to care about him so they could talk about Ava. It was all about her and it always would be. He wanted rid of this man, and found himself hoping that his mum would arrive to make it happen.

"Low even for you, De Rossi." The other reporter was in the doorway now. They didn't like each other, that much was clear. Brad remembered that he had been kind to him the day before. He watched as Richard had spoken closely to Paul. Whatever he said worked, and Paul left the room, albeit laughing as he went.

"Is your Mum around, Brad?" Richard looked a bit pale, and held onto the chair for support. Brad pointed through the wall.

"Thanks." Richard said. He made to leave but turned back. "It's all going to be okay, you know." Brad nodded.

Richard wasn't sure why he had felt the need to comfort the young man. Maybe he was trying to speak something into existence, more for himself than anybody else. He went in search of Tara, following the deep breaths and spitting sounds. How much could he trust her? Ava had, and that had been enough to him before, but now he didn't know what to think. Anyway, he had the feeling that how trustworthy he was would be the deciding factor of any conversation and not the other way around.

"Still struggling?" He asked, as if it wasn't obvious. Tara simply nodded. "I need to piece together what happened last night – I thought we might give it a shot together?"

At this, she picked herself up using the toilet bowl. They moved into the bedroom together, Tara taking cautious steps with Richard being ready to catch her should she collapse, which did look likely.

"I'm so ashamed of myself. I never get like that." She said, lying down on the bed. Richard imagined that she would never act so casual in company, but the fight was out of her.

"I think it's safe to say that it was a bit out of your control."

"Maybe you're right, but I was drunk already. *That's* unlike me." Tara admitted.

"And you were getting your own drinks up until then?"

She nodded in response, knowing where he's going.

"I remember accepting drinks from lots of people, and I've got a feeling that their faces aren't going to become any clearer."

"Can you name any at all?" Richard asked.

"Just Brad." Tara said, shrugging to show that she didn't even consider an option her son could have spiked her. Richard bit his tongue and banked the information for later. Now wasn't the time to question their relationship if he wanted a friend on the island.

"You say you never get like that – what was different last night?" Richard's questions were delivered casually.

"Ava was different. Usually there would be a million things for me to do, but she kept telling me to take the night off, that today would be a big day."

"Today?"

Tara nodded. She had managed to lift her head enough to meet the bottle of water she was holding with a shaky hand.

"She was going to announce something. For the first time since I've known her, she hadn't told me what it was." She said.

"Did anybody else know this?" Richard leant forward, hoping that it would spur his mind to do something similar. It didn't.

"David, I guess. And anybody else she told last night. I wouldn't be surprised if she did – usually she couldn't hold her water. That's why it was so intriguing this time. I guess I tried a bit too hard to forget about it for the night."

"A business move, you reckon?"

"Who knows. Although if it was, I think she would've told me." Tara said, almost defensively.

"Why's that?"

Tara seemed to hesitate as she realised the detectives would eventually pull at this same thread. Her sickness had left no room for worry up until this point.

"Well, a while ago she asked me to take control of the company." She said.

For the first time, Tara found the strength to sit up and look at Richard. She wanted to see his reaction.

"You were the one she sold her shares to?" He asked, trying his best to keep it light.

"Yes." Tara said with a mixture of guilt and defiance.

With that Richard's list of who he could trust on the island may have reduced from one to zero, but he saw no reason to suspect Tara on that alone. Deep down he was relieved that the heat might be taken off him slightly, but he condemned himself for that.

"Listen, let's focus on last night. Before your drink was spiked, do you remember anybody acting strange?"

Tara arched her eyebrows at the daft question – if she had she would be shouting it from the rooftop.

"Yeah, me neither." Richard admitted. "Anyone you were surprised to see invited?"

"Most people. Hayley, for one. That journalist that she hates – not you." Tara smiled but it disappeared as quick as it came. "The rest I could probably justify, all people she's worked with over the years or saw herself working with soon."

"What about Bobby Taggart?"

"He's just everywhere. No surprise really."

Richard racked his brains for anyone else of note, but couldn't come up with anything. That meant that his next call would be either De Rossi or Hayley. It didn't feel like a step in the right direction – more like shuffling on the spot.

"Whatever she was planning, she must've known that I would've tried to talk her out of it. That's the only reason she wouldn't tell me." Tara offered, seemingly finally over the worse of the hangover.

"So the question is what could she do that you wouldn't approve of?" Richard said, moving to the window and looking out to the ocean. It was choppy from a strong wind picking up. He kept an eye on Tara in the reflection, who was in deep thought.

"I have no idea." She said.

The number of people Richard had interviewed in his career reached into triple digits. Some of them he liked, some of them he despised and some he couldn't care less about. Some had told the truth without much prompting, others had held onto it for as long as they could, eventually spilling it like a heavy bucket of water they had to carry on their shoulders. Some, however, had lied to him. He wouldn't be able to put into words how he knew, but he did. He could now add Tara to that list.

"Whatever happened to page 3?" Bobby Taggart joined Paul De Rossi, who was now basking in the sun on the beanbag chairs.

"Times change." De Rossi said, accepting the coffee that he held his way.

"Shame." Bobby crossed one leg over the other, seemingly out of small talk already.

"We're a bit young to be reminiscing about the good old days, don't you think?"

"You're right – it's the near future I've come to talk about."
De Rossi took a sip of the drink – it was a cappuccino, which he had never liked, but if Bobby Taggert offered you a warm cup of spit you pretended to appreciate it.

"You'll be writing a story about this I assume?" Bobby continued.

"I think it would be a crying shame to let it go untold, don't you?"

"Indeed." Bobby finished his own drink and laid the mug on the grass. Someone would get it, he was sure. "Well you'll need someone to cast some suspicion on. Won't sell many papers otherwise, will you?"

"Go on."

"I think our friend Richard Dickson may be a smart choice, until our boys in blue do their work."

De Rossi looked past Bobby. Could he do that to one of his own? Dickson was quick enough to disassociate himself from the tabloids, so was it really against the code? Was there even a code anymore? Journalism was on its knees – loyalties and dignity had gone out the window a long time ago. So the fact that Richard was a colleague wasn't a problem – but what about the morality in general? It wouldn't be the first time he had put someone in the firing line to make his life easier, whether they deserved it or not. There was also the small matter of arguably one of the most powerful men in the country asking a favour of him.

"And if I ask what's in it for you?" De Rossi said.

Bobby Taggart laughed at this – a pompous, privately educated snigger.

"Then you'd be asking the wrong thing. I'd suggest considering what's in it for *you*." He responded.

De Rossi said nothing back. Yes, he had mastered running his mouth, but he also knew the right time to keep it shut. He had a feeling that he'd be on page 3 soon, and plenty more. Plus, as some one the island were well aware, it wouldn't be the first time he had accepted a morally corrupt deal to further his career and he was determined to make sure it wouldn't be the last either.

20

DS Donnelly was having a hard time convincing herself that the badge she had found on the beach was a clue, never mind convincing DI Rankin. Still, the sum of everything else offered was the square root of zero, so she searched the phrase 're-empower' on her phone in the hope of a break. The results that popped up were absolutely useless. Business coaching courses, a personal care brand with two followers on Twitter and various uses of the word that didn't even appear to be dictionary defined. Was that what intrigued her in the first place? She had known that it wasn't a word, or certainly not a common one. Maybe the fact that it was hardly used online was something to ponder. Still, to take it to her superior would require something more. What did it mean to her? To fix something that was once broken. To rise from a pit you had been forced into. To come back stronger despite where you'd been. Yes definitely not something to take to Rankin yet – she could hear him now *"You're saying she's going to come back from the dead? Get some real work done, Sharon."* She cursed him in her head for something that he hadn't yet said. Using her first name like that he was her father? The cheek. God, she needed a drink.

"Anything?" As if by magic, Rankin now stood over her. He had tasked her with looking into Richard Dickson's relationship with Ava.

"Nothing that solves a murder case unfortunately."

"But it might send us on the right path."

DS Donnelly clicked open some tabs on her laptop.

"They went to the same high school together – and had a brief romantic relationship. It ended when Ava was whisked away to stardom. From what we've heard, they kept in touch here and there throughout the years, but certainly weren't close. Maybe he held some ill feelings about her success and leaving him behind?" She asked, but Rankin took it as rhetorical, and waved his hands to urge her to continue. "That's it, sir. The next thing, she invited him here. He's in the middle of a scandal so it does seem a strange one."

"Gareth Young." Rankin nodded.

"Yes, the politician who sexually assaulted his speech writer."

"Allegedly." Her superior pointed out.

"Allegedly." She agreed, begrudgingly.

"What's his story? Why's he never written about her? Seems like a match made in heaven." Rankin pulled up a chair now, confirming to Donnelly that he had little else to go on.

"He tends to focus on more *important* topics." At this, she did air quotes.

"Such as?"

"Started out exposing local town issues, moved onto corrupt business practices, now in the world of politics and the rich and famous. A squeaky clean voice for good with an axe to grind."

"Show me someone who's never done anything wrong and I'll show you a good liar."

"Agreed." Said DS Donnelly, who had taken an immediate dislike to Richard. In fact, she had disliked him ever since the Gareth Young story. Another man bursting in and trying to save the day and messing up. Who suffers? The woman, again. She also wondered why exactly he was here. To her, it seemed like a courtesy invite that Ava assumed wouldn't have been accepted. But it was accepted, and here he came with all of his problems and tension. It wasn't only Richard who she had a feeling about. The PA woman – Tara – was a strange one. Okay, she had to pause the questioning at two points to vomit, but beyond that, there was something she had been hiding. DS Donnelly was good at picking up signs. Tara had lied about her age – she knew that for fact. When she did, she ran her fingertip across her eyelid. She did this again three times. Once when asked if she would call her son's upbringing normal. The second time was when she said she thought that the transferring of company ownership to her name was coincidental, and the third was when Donnelly had asked her if she had kept secrets for Ava. Tara had said no, but her finger said differently.

"What about the other esteemed member of our fourth estate - the fake Italian?" DI Rankin interrupted her thoughts.

"You could fertilise acres with the amount of bullshit he's produced over the years."

"Any potential for a grudge there?" He asked.

"Apparently Ava was going to stop giving him quotes, and stop any sources speaking to him. Something about moving away from a toxic culture. Doubt it would've stopped him writing it anyway." Donnelly responded, making sure that her superior was taking it all in.

"And his coverage of her up until now – positive? Negative?"

"A bit of both really. You know how it goes, they have their targets. Sometimes it was Ava Hart, sometimes it wasn't." DI Rankin seemed to be out of questions, so Donnelly continued. "One thing that is interesting is the access he seems to have to sources. It seems there isn't a person on this island that he hasn't written about in detail. I reckon he knows more than he's letting on."

DI Rankin nodded, confirming the points' relative importance. Although, it was the other journalist he was interested in finding out more about.

It was hard to catch Hayley's attention in between phone calls, but Richard bided his time. He knew that he had to start making some steps forward if he was going to get DI Rankin off his back. He stood even closer to the model and superstar, letting her know that he was up next whether the phone rang or not. She seemed to be dragging out the end of her conversation to avoid what was to come. Finally hanging up, Hayley looked at Richard. Richard recognised it as what one might call resting bitch face. Her upper lip was curved slightly as if there was something that smelled bad on it. Just like an OCD child's colouring book, none of Hayley's make up went outside the lines.

"Yes?" She said, showing even more contempt for him than he had expected.

"Have I done something to offend you?" He asked, seeing no reason to seek her approval.

"People are talking." She said, simply. It was enough to tell him everything he needed to know.

"I had nothing to do with Ava's death, if that's what you mean."

Hayley didn't reply, she just waited for him to get to his point.

"I did see you having a pretty heated conversation with her though – so you shouldn't be so quick to judge." He continued.

"It's none of your business, but we were actually clearing the air." She said.

"Right. And your plan to steal her manager – was that part of the new friendship?"

Hayley tried her best to hide the surprise.

"Who told you that?"

"People are talking." Richard imitated. He didn't mention that overhearing the conversation between Hayley and David was one of the few things he remembered from the night before.

"Not that I have to explain myself, but that was all David. To be honest, I've not even decided if I'll take him up on it. Probably not, considering..."

"Might not be a good look just now." Richard agreed, hoping that she was warming to him. She wasn't.

"You never know – he's probably thinking the same thing." He continued.

"I'm sure one of his skivvies will stop by to let me know soon." Hayley rolled her eyes as she spoke.

"He wouldn't tell you himself?"

"David doesn't do *anything* himself – pair that with countless people wanting into his good books and he has himself a nice little team."

"He seems quite hands on to me." Richard said. Hayley gave a sniff of approval at his joke, but that was all.

She was thinking now, ignoring his presence. The decision to go with David had seemed obvious the night before – he was a ruthless manager and they had a good relationship before. Now, it could be career ending. Richard noticed a flicker of light from her fingers. Hayley was turning a golden rectangle in her hand. It took a few turns for Richard to be able to see what it said. Finally, he read RE-EMPOWER.

"Can I ask you something?" He said. Hayley broke from her trance and nodded. She put the badge back in her pocket. "You don't really think I did it, do you?"

"It's Richard isn't it?" She knew fine well that it was. Richard could imagine that she used that tactic often. He nodded. "If you lined up everyone on this island, could you really point out a murderer? Drug addicts – yes. Tax fraudsters – of course. Child abusers? Probably. A murderer? I can't see it, but there is one. They say it's always who you least suspect – so what happens when you suspect everyone as little as the next person? All bets are off."

"So you're saying it has to be someone, and that turns out to be me?"

"Right now, you seem to be *trending*, as they say."

Richard could see the same logical thinking and savvy that Ava had when he looked at Hayley. It made him feel slightly better about celebrity culture - these people weren't just falling into being rich and famous. Hayley looked at Richard as another call was coming in. He nodded his thanks for her time and she turned away. He caught a glimpse of her tanned leg.

"We didn't spend the night together last night, did we?" He asked. It was good to see Hayley laugh, even if it was at him and in his face. "No. Makes sense." He said as she answered the call.

Richard walked slowly in no particular direction, claustrophobia creeping in despite his surroundings being so vast. Hayley was right – it was hard to picture anyone here as a killer. Putting himself in the mind of others, he could see why the weird guy from Ava's past currently in a whirlwind of scandal might be the most suspicious. Were the police really following him as their main lead? What about fingerprints? Everybody on the island had probably touched Ava throughout the night. Had he really been the only person not able to confirm an alibi? No, someone must be lying, or being helped. His own suspicions were changing with every conversation he had. He hadn't even begun to think about who had spiked his drink – and why did they target just him and Tara? There could be more around that had fallen victim to it and were just treating it like a bad hangover. It must've been the same person who had tampered with both drinks. Did that mean it was Brad? No, he was certain that he hadn't spoken to him at all at the party. Could he have asked someone else to give it to Richard? Maybe, and deep-down Richard still felt there was something strange about the young man – like he was acting sad. According to Tara Ava was like a sister to him, but siblings could fall out bitterly. The fact that Richard still couldn't paint a clear picture of Ava in his head was a source of guilt – once so close, even lovers, and he didn't know enough about her to begin to work out the motivations behind her killing. Tara could shed some light, but she had already lied to him once. After avoiding one another since arriving on the island, Richard thought that it was high time that he should be meeting David. First, he'd find out what else the search engines had to say about him.

21

Richard snapped his laptop shut out of a mixture of frustration and secrecy. The strange looks he was getting around the island had doubled then doubled again. His paranoia told him that soon everyone here would be staring at him, even the killer. It was the sort of cruel irony you might smile at if it was in a film. He waited for the group of women to pass behind him before flipping open the screen again. He didn't care about people suspecting him but didn't want to do anything to give it more velocity. Still, the moment the police wanted to arrest him, they would. The more he thought about it the more certain he was that Rankin had him as number one suspect, and the man was slowly becoming feral in the pursuit of a result. It was in Richard's power and his power alone to find a thread to the story worth pulling to clear his name. And there lay the trouble...

There was no doubt that Ava held grudges. He had discovered now that it was hard to find an interview with her where she didn't have some heavily masked dig at a person or group of people, always perfectly veiled to not lead to any identification. So why was she doing it? Was she letting people somebody know that one day she would reveal all? Or was she simply toying with them? It could just be for clicks, or maybe it was that twisted sense of humour that Richard remembered from their school years – the one that would never send him into convulsions of laughter again. He was on page 15 of the image results, finding nothing but comfort in seeing Ava full of life once more, although nothing would ever replace the image of her body on the beach. Like a squiggle of light in his eye, that would be in his vision forever, always teasing to reveal itself. If the pictures weren't of Ava on her own, David and Tara would be in them. Tara's tongue would usually be parting her lips ever so slightly – a giveaway that she was concentrating on making sure wherever Ava was and whatever she was doing was going according to schedule. David didn't seem to be there for any other reason than to have one eye on Ava. In different circumstances, Richard would find it pathetic rather than sinister. He flicked through a few more pictures. Without fail, if her manager was featured he'd be almost out of the frame and looking over at her. Never smiling.

"Lunatic." Herb stumbled over in a zig zag pattern like a man failing a roadside sobriety test. "Lunatic." This time he said it louder and angled his mouth over his shoulder. He was nursing a red eye.

"Snap." Richard said, pointing to it and making Herb aware of his presence. Herb looked back once more to make sure that the altercation was over. He puffed out laboured breaths but held his frame high. Despite his advancing years, he looked fit.

"I've said it since day one – he's trouble. About as much dignity as a dog with diarrhoea." His Northern accent made everything sound like a common saying. Richard was sure that wasn't one, but he let him vent. "Attacking me? And having it broken up before I could get a shot back? The coward."

It seemed he was talking to himself more than anything else, but finally his eyes settled on Richard. He gave a kind smile as if he knew nothing else but good, old-fashioned manners.

"Who was it?" Richard asked.

"David *fucking* Morgan. Who else? The only little man who's done any harm on this island, but they refuse to see it."

"The police?"

"Everybody – they're all that far up his arse that I'm surprised he's not taller. Mark my words, son, he controlled Ava in life and he –" Herb couldn't bring himself to finish the sentence, but the point was clear. For Richard, it was validation of a growing hunch but nothing concrete just yet. The last thing he wanted to do was falsely accuse anyone of anything – he still had the bruises from last time. On top of all of that, Herb was foaming at mouth with rage – a sign accepted worldwide of someone out of their mind.

"Take a seat." Richard said, placing his laptop to his left. Maybe Herb would offer more insight than the internet could. The hefty man flattened the grass beside him like a cow before the rain, and with just as much dignity.

"How did it start?" Richard asked, sizing up Herb's shiner and comparing it to his own. It was nowhere near as bad, already returning to its normal size and losing a bit of redness.

"We've never got on, him and I. Similar ages, same circles, jobs are shades of the one colour, but we couldn't be more different."

"In what ways?"

"How we use the little power that we have, I suppose."

"Little? Doesn't seem like that from the outside."

"Being the most important person in a room all depends on the room, son." Herb pointed out.

Son. There it was again. It was almost a tic that he had. Richard felt strange about it – both warm and patronised at the same time.

"You've known him all these years?"

"It's usually easier than this to keep our distance."

"You'd think Ava would've known to keep you apart." Mentioning her seemed inappropriate. Richard wondered how long that would last for.

"You'd think." Herb agreed

"But they were close?"

"We're all close to an arsehole, son – that's just basic biology."

"Did it irritate you that she didn't see what you see in him?"

"All the time. But he had her from that young age. His first star. He got his claws in before she could harden to his sort of sleaze." Herb paused and took a breath.

"She must've seen something in him to stay beside him all those years." Richard said.

Herb didn't take it as a question and let the breeze fill the space between them. Richard could hear the man's breath returning to calm levels – he didn't seem the fighting type, more calm and composed. Despite this, Herb seemed to carry hurt with him. It wasn't hard for Richard to spot – a bit like masons and their handshakes, injured souls can spot one another. Spotting it was easy but finding out what was a puzzle that could rarely be solved without some hints along the way. He figured that Herb, in his moment of fragility, might be most likely to open up now.

"You married, Herb?"

"Not for me."

"Kids?"

He paused and then shook his head as if he couldn't think of anything worse. Two strikes. Perhaps the turmoil was fresher.

"Did you introduce them? Ava and David?" Richard asked, knowing that an affirmative answer would be progress. Herb gave the slightest nod, wincing with pain and holding his eye to pretend that's where it was coming from.

"And you regret it?" He continued.

"Every single day."Herb turned his face towards the beach as if he was hiding tears. "Listen, I don't want to see any of this in tomorrow's papers."

"I'm not working on a story." Richard said.

"I know – I'm just making sure. Let the police do their job. Still, I wouldn't blame you for taking it into your own hands."

"So you're saying you want it out there? Or not?"

"No, no. Not for me to decide a man's fate like that. He's rotten to the core though. I can smell it. And the media holds all the power nowadays, don't you? Loudest voice in the room." Herb said. Richard thought about it. He certainly didn't feel powerful. In fact, he was close to shutting down.

"Depends on the size of the room." He said, taking his cigarettes from his pocket and scanning the island for David.

Tara flinched as the door slammed. There was no calming him down when he was like this. When he was a child it was annoying, but as he had grown into a young man it became scary. She took another sip of water and gulped, determined to not show Brad her fear. The day that happened their relationship would change forever. She loved him deeply, but his nasty temper was hard to justify. He opened the door and came back out shouting again.

"I want to go!"

"Bradley, we simply can't. We'll be here until the police do what they have to do." Tara kept her voice low, hoping he would mirror it. He didn't.

"Even when she's dead she's controlling our lives." Brad spat.

Tara had flashes of the night Ava died and a shouting match with Brad. Maybe that could explain some of the looks they were getting around the island. The memory was fleeting and dreamlike. Tara couldn't decide whether or not she preferred it that way.

"She didn't even want me around." Brad said, lowering his voice slightly.

"You and I both know that's not true."

"Mum, she only put up with me so you'd do all the stuff she thought she was too good to do."

Tara felt her hand raise but forced it back down. She had never struck him and wasn't about to start. Plus, she knew it would be a fight she would lose, especially when he was like this. Could he hurt her? Did he have it in him? The question terrified her, because she was pretty sure she knew that answer.

"And you know what?" Brad shouted as he walked away. Tara knew exactly what was coming. "I'm glad she's dead."

He slammed the door, shaking the cheap watercolours on the wall. Tara turned and leant on the bannister. She shut her eyes tightly and pictured Ava, and what she would say to her now if she had the chance. *This was all your fault. Everything was your fault.* As her tears began to tickle her cheeks, Tara opened her eyes and was greeted by the female detective, Donnelly, at the bottom of the stairs. Her look was one of sympathy, although Tara couldn't tell if it was to say *kids eh?* Or *your son is on his way to being arrested right in front of you.* Either way, she broke eye contact quickly and went into her room. She knew he wouldn't be cooling off, only stewing further, but there was nothing she could do. It was sadly ironic that the only person who could speak to him in that state had been Ava – another quirk of their complicated relationship. She had incredible patience for him, even more so than Tara. Only once did Tara witness Ava lose her temper with Brad. She had caught him spying on her in the shower a few years back when puberty had grabbed him and shook him violently, causing a growth spurt and the introduction of sexual curiosity. Ava, almost always composed, went ballistic. Brad was painfully embarrassed by the whole thing, and his already bubbling resentment for her could only spill over. They had balled at each other that night.

Tara woke up her tablet, aware that it had been pinging all morning with what she expected would be emails of condolence and shock. She couldn't face them – not yet. Instead, she opened her spreadsheet of the guests. Even within catastrophe, the sharp lines and clear boxes of the perfectly formed spreadsheet soothed her. She could control this. She could process it. As was her way, she knew for a fact that there were no unexpected arrivals. With that considered, the name of Ava's murderer was on the screen in front of her – the only problem was that it was hidden within around 200 others. She made sure not to let her eyes focus on Brad's name for more than a few seconds. Beside him was David – a man Tara had always felt exploited Ava for personal gain, but that was the reason that she would struggle to suspect him of killing her. What could he gain from it? Unless she was about to reveal how he really was, which would be a shock to many. But why would Ava do that? She considered a few more names before closing the window in frustration. As she went to put it off, her eyes were drawn to a picture of Ava in the top right corner of the screen. It wasn't a paparazzi shot, or one from a photoshoot – just a selfie taken with the tablet's camera. She was blessed with the kind of looks that never peak – every year she seemed to be more beautiful. Tara always wondered at what age the trajectory would change downwards, but she would never know now. She clicked on the picture and the background changed – she was in Ava's profile now, one they had set up on a long trip where her own laptop had given up and packed in. Ava hadn't used the device in over a year, but her cloud login was still active. At her fingertips, Tara had access to all of her documents, but that was nothing new and she didn't expect to find a note. What she did find, however, was a diary. For a period of about 4 months, Ava had a weekly column in a woman's mag written in the form of a diary. Of course it was carefully put together to get that week's endorsement and name drop in, but Tara remember her saying that she found it therapeutic. As with many other hobbies, Tara assumed that it would last only for a flicker of time. As she clicked it open, she was proved wrong. The last entry was the night before the party. Tara's tears returned as she read the last words Ava would ever write. *Most of all, I wish I hadn't put Tara though all of this.*

22

"Scared?" David stood beside the small speedboat that was anchored to a wooden post that looked hundreds of years old.

"I just saw the bruises you gave to the last guy you spoke to, so you'll forgive my hesitancy." Richard replied.

"Him? An absolute clown of a man – sometimes he needs reminding that he's no better than the rest of us."

"And who gave you that role?"

"Nobody's ever given me anything." David's confidence sounded like childish arrogance.

"Might look a bit suspicious, going off the island, no?" Richard said, arriving at the boat.

"I don't know about you, but I've got nothing to hide."

At this, and to show that he didn't either, Richard nodded and moved towards the vessel. Together, they pushed it out further into the shallows. Water lapped at the bottom of Richard's jeans, and a cold breeze accentuated the feeling. He was desperate for a shower, or a scalding hot bath – immersing his head beneath the surface so that all that was there was Mary's presence.

David started the small engine, seemingly having done it before. Richard knew that if he wanted to find out anything about David Morgan that he would have to do it on his terms. He stepped aboard the boat, bringing the looped rope with him. David smiled at his small victory and started the engine, drowning any uncomfortable silence that was on the horizon. Beginning to circle the island's orbit, Richard took in its vastness once more. It was a stunning place, now forever to be scarred with Ava's death like a beautiful painting with an ink spill stretching across it. The derelict castle came into view. David switched off the engine and they bobbed with the current. After the noise, the silence was noticeable. Alongside him for the first time in such a small space, Richard began to notice details about David that he had previously missed. Although he appeared calm overall, a closer inspection showed various slight movements and tics. Dilated pupils surrounded by bloodshot whites looked like lightning striking an oil spill. Everything pointed to a cocaine addiction, which was more of a cliché than a surprise. David put his sunglasses on.

"It feels like you've something to ask me." David said, masking his impatience relatively well. They were standing in the kind of proximity that only usually ended up in a kiss or a fight, so Richard sat down. David followed his lead.

"What did she mean to you?"

"More than she meant to you, stranger. I've been here for the last 20 years – you?"

"Sometimes presence isn't a good thing."

David ignored this, seemingly not one to get into verbal sparring, so Richard continued.

"Rumours are that the two of you dated." He said.

"Right back at you." David replied.

"Yeah, and I don't make a habit of avoiding that fact. So did you?"

"Anything I tell you ends up on the front page as a part of your comeback story. You think I'm about to help you with that?" David finished and stood up from the small plastic bench, looking towards the castle. His low centre of gravity made him stay steady as the boat dipped and rocked from side to side. Richard decided to stay sitting, but looked in the same direction. The castle was a status above ruins, with some rooms appearing to be intact. Others were halfway off the cliff or reduced to rubble. It was putting up a good fight, but one that it would ultimately lose. He tried not to be symbolic.

"You don't seem too upset about her death." Richard pointed out. He wanted to see how David would react.

"I've seen a lot in this business – I suppose I'm hardened to it."

"Even murder?"

"Death, yes. Murder, no." He shrugged, unable to explain.

"You knew Ava was on the same path that others have been on? On her way to some sort of crisis?"

"There are no paths, Dick, just conveyor belts."

"And you're in control of them." Richard finished the exchange. David didn't dignify it with a response.

The silence started to make Richard feel uneasy. How could Ava's manager – and a career long one at that – be so cold in the situation? And why wasn't he pretending not to be? Deep in his thoughts, Richard hadn't noticed that David's gaze had settled onto him. Or at least he guessed it had, but it was hard to tell through the dark lenses.

"What do you think happened to her?" He asked, aware that with the sunglasses on he wouldn't be able to spot any tell-tale signs of a lie.

"Off the record?" David said.

"Assuming it's not a confession."

David wanted to knock him off the boat, that much was clear. He loosened his fist though and chose his words slowly.

"You're looking for answers? There's only one person on this island who knows everything there is to know about Ava. If she's not involved, she knows who is."

"Tara?"

"We have a winner." David said, twirling his finger sarcastically.

"The only problem is that the killer thought the same. Her drink was spiked." Richard told him.

"How convenient." David mused. "And I suppose her little demon was accounted for as well?"

"Brad's not a good kid?"

"Brad's a weird kid. Doesn't make him bad I suppose – but the arguments he caused between the two of them were the only time I've ever seen Ava angry."

"You saw them?"

"Heard them mostly. Through hotel walls, on planes – stuff

like that." It was clear that Davide enjoyed gossiping, as much as he knew that it wouldn't be in his best interest.

"And they were always about Brad?" Richard asked.

"Sounded like it to me. Anyway, I tend to avoid anything to do with him. Believe it or not a single man hanging around a 17-year-old kid is no longer a good look in our industry."

"It didn't stop you with Ava." Richard said, willing the words to go unheard as soon as they were spoken.

David took his sunglasses off and stared into his eyes, not doing well to hide the pulses of rage making their way through his body. He reached back and started the engine. As he lead them dangerously back to shore, his muscles twitched and jaw clenched. Richard turned and looked towards the island, desperate not to show fear. He calmed himself by remembering what Hayley had said. David may have been the one in charge, but he had people to do his dirty work. Maybe Richard's search for an impassioned killer was the wrong road. Maybe it was all more calculated. For now, all he could concentrate on was not becoming the second victim in the few minutes it would take to reach land.

Tara scrolled back through the diary. She knew almost everything already, but reading it through Ava's tinted view was interesting. As she took it in, there were moments that she forgot her friend was dead. It made it hurt more when real life took hold again. She read on.

Tara signed the papers today. I could see her hand shaking from a mile but pretended to look away. One perfect squiggle and she was set for life – holding the kind of fortune that little girls dream of from school age. I know I did. It's hard to pin point a time that I realised it meant nothing. People who have money are forever telling those who don't that it isn't everything. I'm not that idiotic, but it's true in part. The lawyer asked me in private why I was giving her it all – not just what I have now, but what I'll make in the future. Where do I start? Plus, we're connected in a way that nobody would under-

stand but us. What's hers is mine, and vice versa. Tara, if you've stumbled on this looking for a spreadsheet – hi. Stop doing that weird smile, it makes you look like you need the toilet. Sometimes I want to ask you to forgive me for putting you in this position, even though it may seem like a good one to someone on the outside looking in. You're probably pursing your lips now and thinking that I'm being daft after a couple of glasses of wine. You may be right. You and Brad will never want for anything. I know I've made it complicated for you both, and I promise I'm working a way out to give you something close to normal. It breaks my heart that he resents me, and that you might one day too. Just promise you'll let me visit, yeah? Or maybe you'll never read this at all.

Tears cascaded from Tara's cheeks and hit screen. She let them fall and smiled at the strange idea of being away from Ava long enough that when they met again it would be considered a visit. Small talk, offers of coffee or some wine. What she would give for it to be a possibility.

23

Brad was pinching the skin on his thigh. He thought maybe it would cause a few tears. They might cut the interview short if he cried.

"You still with us, son?" DI Rankin said in his gruff voice. Brad didn't like him.

"Yeah. Sorry."

"It's important you tell us everything you can remember from last night, Brad. We want to find the person who did this to your Mum's friend."

"She was her boss." Brad said. "But okay – I'll try." He had already admitted to being drunk, they reminded him that he was underage but didn't seem to care too much. He got the feeling that they had spoken to him for longer than anyone else. Why? What did they know?

"Go on." Rankin said, losing patience.

"I was dancing." Brad looked embarrassed to even say the word. He knew the two detectives would be picturing his lanky frame waving his long arms like Mr Tickle. He was sure he saw DI Rankin stifle a smirk. "Not really dancing, but I was with people who were. Just talking and having a good time. They were telling stories. I didn't have much to tell, but they seemed okay with me being there."

"Was Ava there?"

"No. In fact, the stories were mostly about her. Quite nasty stuff. Stupid stuff like who she had slept with, and who she had stabbed in the back. Things like that that don't really matter."

"Why do you think they don't matter?" DS Donnelly said. He liked her – she had a nice smile.

"Everyone does it, don't they? Have sex, fall out, act horrible to people."

"Did anybody act horrible to you?"

"I'm nearly eighteen you know. I'm not a kid." Brad said. Her smile seemed patronising now. He knew that neither of them was a friend.

"Okay, I know." DS Donnelly said. "It's just it might give us an idea of who to look more closely at."

"Everybody was nice. Some of the men made jokes and made me get drinks for them, but that was it."

"Who did you get drinks for?"

Brad shrugged, knowing fine well that he gave one to his mum but didn't remember who told him to do it. He didn't have a hangover, or at least this isn't what he imagined one would be like, but his memory was hazy.

"If you could try and remember that would be a big help." DI Rankin said through his teeth. Brad nodded.

"So what did you do after the dancing?" DS Donnelly asked.

"My mum was all over the place. Embarrassing herself. I helped her up to bed."

"Some people have told us that they heard some shouting. Was that you?" Donnelly said, with her gaze focused on the teen.

Brad considered lying, really considered it. This was the moment he had practiced in the mirror – the moment that they would start to suspect him. Ava had taught him a lot of lessons, probably more than his mum had. Amongst them was that if you were going to lie, make it temporary. She had said that not telling the truth was okay if you thought it was for the best, but you always had to one day. Maybe it was for the best if he just kept it to himself for now...

"DS Donnelly is a bit nicer than I am, Brad. We already know it was you. We know you and your mum had a screaming match and once she passed out you left the house. It'll be easier for everyone if you just tell us where you went." DI Rankin had him locked in his sights now. The tears started to come, and he didn't have to hurt himself this time. They were hot on his cheeks. He thought they might offer him a minute to compose himself, but no. DI Ranking was on his feet now.

"Where did you go, Brad?" He wasn't quite shouting, but it was close enough.

At this point, Tara burst into the room.

"Miss Scott, if you could please wait outside." DS Donnelly said, but Brad sensed some understanding in her tone.

"Don't shout at him." Tara said, moving towards the table. "I'm allowed to be with him, and maybe we should have a lawyer."

"Where did you go Brad?" Rankin's eyes were bulging.

"I didn't kill her!" Brad shouted "I went for a walk to clear my head, that was all I swear."

"Anywhere near the cliffs that Ava was thrown from?"

"No!" Brad was sobbing now. Tara put her arm around him, but he shrugged it off violently. "Leave me alone. It's your fault we're here."

Tara slotted her arm around her chest and said nothing.

"I think it's best if we leave it for now. Brad, it's important that you remember everything you can and tell us. We'll pick this up again." DS Donnelly looked at her superior for his approval. He nodded and turned away from the table. He didn't turn back to address Brad as he made for the door.

"You wouldn't mind leaving your phone with us, would you son?"

"My phone?" Brad replied, a shake in his voice.

"Those things people used to use to call people."

"Why do you want my phone? No."

That was all Rankin needed. He turned round at this point, now sporting a smug smile.

"Take a seat and I'll organise the paperwork so we can take it then. It won't take long."

"Bradley..." Tara said, but her tone wasn't convincing, partly because she felt a deep dread about why he would refuse in the first place. She wanted to tell him to hand it over but her instincts stopped her. How had it come to this? How could she possibly suspect him of killing Ava?

"I enjoy silence as much as the next man, but we've got an investigation to be getting on with. Your phone." Rankin nodded to the table that split the room. Brad looked at Tara for support but she stared into space. He took it from his pocket and let it fall onto the desk, giving it a few inches of a drop and praying that it would scramble the tech enough to break it. It didn't.

"There's a good lad." Rankin said. "Now do me a favour and scribble the code down for us. Donnelly placed a blank shred of paper on the table and handed Brad a pen. She noted the shake of his hand and the moistness of his palm. Brad wrote the six numbers down and left the room. Before Tara followed, she turned to the detectives.

"I wish I could remember more, but I know my son and you're wrong if you think he had anything to do with this." She said, tears now forming in her eyes as well. DS Donnelly nodded, more of a dismissal than an agreement.

When they were alone, Donnelly could hear Rankin's breathing. His temper had gotten the better of him there, she had seen it bubbling since they had arrived on the island. Now though, with Brad's phone, his spirits were lifted. She picked it up but didn't look at the screen just yet. Instead, she watched from the window as Brad left the house. A troubled teen, no doubt about it. He deserved a normal life, maybe counselling. And yet, all of the sympathy in the world couldn't change the fact that he might be a murderer. Like turning the final page of a novel, part of her really didn't want to continue.

Richard had stayed on the beach as David returned to the campsite, sitting in the sun as it began to set on what was a day filled with tragedy and confusion. More than ever he felt he had to tell Ava's story. If anything, it would be personal therapy. Nobody would have to read it. He picked up a handful of sand and stones and let it all fall through his fingertips. How much of it still had some traces of Ava? The visual of her lifeless body – one that he had been fighting from his mind all day – returned.

In death she had looked delicate and vulnerable, the opposite of how Richard thought of her. In the past, deaths he had experienced were always framed by selfish thoughts. When his sister was killed, he cursed himself for still being alive without her. When his mother died, he felt sorry for himself, and constantly wondered how he would go on without her guiding light. With Ava, and for the first time, nothing about him entered his mind. He thought of all she did and all she was meant to go on to do, of how many young women she had entertained and inspired. He thought of her parents, who were now experiencing the same thing as his own had – losing a child well before it was fair. Richard didn't want Ava's memory to be reduced to a heartstrings headline, or emotional porn for readers to digest and forget about. He didn't want to capitalise on it one bit. The trouble was, if he didn't, someone else would. As if by the gods of journalism, Paul De Rossi stepped onto the beach and towered over Richard.

"Sorry to have to do this, Dickson." He said, pen and pad poised.

"Do what?" Richard squinted up at his doughy silhouette. It took a few seconds before he noticed that he was ready to take notes. He wanted to react in anger, but either exhaustion or realism stopped him. "What's it got to do with me?"

"That's the part I'm sorry for." De Rossi said, going through a process he had hundreds of times before.

"You're putting my name in the mix?" Richard asked, standing now.

"Editor says so. You know the drill." De Rossi said it as if he was about to take an order for the soup of the day rather than a quote from a suspected murderer. Richard considered physical violence, as his temper often made him do. He had enough sense left to make it a last resort, swallowing his anger like a dry pill.

"I refuse to help a scumbag, pathetic excuse for a journalist capitalise on the death of my friend. How's that for a quote?"

"You've got no idea what you're talking about, Dickson."

"No? Enlighten me then. You wrote those stories about her

for her benefit? The bullshit rumours about love affairs, drinking problems, celebrity feuds – you did that all for Ava? Sorry, I never knew you were such a pal." Richard said.

Journalism was awash with hypocrisy; Richard had always known that and he included himself in it. They would encourage others to bare themselves in front of the world to be judged while doing everything they could to remain no more than a name on a byline. Sometimes the name wasn't even real. They were just the messengers. He had recently experienced what it felt like to be on the other side, and it had given him doubts about how he made his money. Of course, all of those worries could be taken from his hands soon, his fate being cemented by this story.

"Let's keep it professional."

"Oh of course, I'm sure your paper will be as professional and respectful as possible. What picture are you leading with – a shot of up Ava's dress?"

At this, De Rossi grabbed Richard's collar with both greasy hands. Up close, Richard could see that he was shaking, his previously unflappable persona faltering with the pressure of the island and its events. Richard stayed calm.

"You feel guilty don't you. About what you're about to do." Richard whispered.

De Rossi tried to hold his stare on Richard but his eyes shot down the way and his grip loosened. Richard took the opportunity to break free, swinging his hands away with more power than he had expected. He moved in close to De Rossi again.

"I never thought I'd see the day that you grew a set of morals." He said, close to his ear. De Rossi's shakes were increasing, as if the ghosts of hundreds of stories were presenting themselves on the beach. But, despite coming close to salvation, he composed himself.

"Those stories you read about her over the years, they pushed it – I don't deny that – but did you ever think that there might be some things I found out that I helped kill?" De Rossi responded, finally.

Killing a story was a common term, but the expression in this context took them both by surprise.

"Whatever helps you sleep at night, De Rossi. Shove your quote up your arse." Richard stepped back, careful not to go too far towards the water. "Just remember that I've got one from you now."

"It's running tomorrow." De Rossi replied, tucking his notepad into his bulging back pocket. "If you've got something to add, find me before 10."

"How worried should I be?" Richard asked.

"We've got nothing concrete. Obviously. But with the public opinion you currently hold, I don't think it will take a lot for some of them to make up their own minds."

Richard had never seen him like this – he had expected him to blame it on his editor, but not for him to actually mean it. He got the feeling that this was a story he really didn't want to write. And yet, he was going to. The problem he had with understanding was that he knew the editor too, and she wasn't one for running something without covering her back. Richard felt almost certain that someone else was pulling De Rossi's strings.

"Do you think I killed her?" He asked, making sure to hold onto De Rossi's stare with his own.

"Honestly? No. But I could say that about everyone else here too."

"And I just fit the narrative?"

De Rossi didn't respond to this, which confirmed that it was true.

"Use my good side, will you?" Richard said, turning to his left slightly and raising his middle finger.

De Rossi turned and made his way towards the hilly path up to the island. There was a big oval of sweat soaking through the back of his shirt. Maybe he wouldn't sleep tonight, or tomorrow, but there was no doubt it would get easier as time went on. Richard didn't bother trying to guess at the amount of lives he had left in ruins as he climbed his way up towards a comfortable living with invites to celebrity parties. He had seen the faces of people before when he mentioned he was a journalist – them automatically assuming that he was the type of person that De Rossi was. The two couldn't be more different, but unfortunately it appeared that they played for the same team. Richard had always thought of De Rossi as an idiot who couldn't string a sentence together without an adjective in all caps like TROUBLED or DISGRACED. Now though, he saw a man in too deep. He seemed powerless, defeated, resigned to the powers that be. Who were those powers? There were some things that he had *helped kill.* Slip of the tongue? Unfortunate coincidence? Richard tried hard to convince himself of either, but in the end he settled on it being more sinister. No, De Rossi's story wasn't just to fill a gap in the papers. It wasn't part of the narrative, or a public service. It was calculated. It was an exercise in deflection, ordered by a killer.

24

"There's something about those two journalists – keep your eye on them." DI Rankin was briefing Chief Inspector Murphy, either ignorant or arrogant to the fact that he was technically ranked beneath him. "We'll be back in the morning, hopefully to wrap this thing up."

Murphy would need some ointment prescribed for the amount of biting his tongue was taking, but he did it again anyway. DS Donnelly, Rankin's right-hand lady, smiled thinly at him as if to apologise. Her superior asked if she had the phone and she patted the inside pocket of her coat. Murphy nodded goodbye and watched them head towards the helicopter. He didn't like seeing such a vehicle on the island – seeing the parting and squashing of the long grass. Still, needs must, it was a murder investigation after all, and for the next 12 or so hours he was in charge as the two townies went to visit the girl's parents. He turned and looked back towards the guests gracing his part of the country. Most had managed to look impeccable despite the lack of the facilities they were used to. Cheryl, his wife of 40 years, only wore a spot of make up on Christmas day, and her cheeks were usually pink from the effort of cooking and hosting anyway. Were these the kind of people his daughter, Chloe, wanted to be like? To be around? Live and let live, he thought, but he hoped she had more sense than that. It was getting dark now, a more forgiving setting for Murphy. As the years piled on top of each other he found his eyes becoming more and more sensitive to bright lights. Not ideal for a police officer. Retirement was coming, that was for sure. He thought of Chloe again, and worried for her. She had moved to London with the strange pairing of wisdom and naivety that only a country girl could have.

Although he wasn't well-versed in murder investigations like this one, he kept an eye on the goings on down south in her area and they made for grim reading. What could he remember about the guilty? They usually fell into one of three camps – gangs, crazy or crazy in love. This had nothing to do with gangs – even the clown Rankin could see that. So that left two options. The crazy ones scared him, of course, but not as much as the ones who had known their victim. Been with them. Stalked them. Knew who they knew, and who they would be hurting by doing what they had planned. He found it hard to think that what had happened here, on this beautiful island, was a crime of passion. The ones who did that usually cracked under the pressure, and there was no pressure quite like being forced to stay at the scene of the crime and observed. So they were looking for someone who knew what they were doing, and thought they had a good chance of getting away with it. If they had no chance they would've cracked by now – admitted it to someone they thought they could trust, or a simply someone with a kind smile. Guilt got the better of the ones who never wanted to do it in the first place – he was sure of it. That boat had sailed with the time that had passed.

Murphy had taken the gender seminars as seriously as everybody else on the force, but no matter how many spectacled gentlemen told him that women were equal, he would bet his pension that their killer was a man. That cut the numbers to around 100 suspects. The odds were similar to his weekly coupon. The chances would increase if anybody, anybody at all, seemed to commit themselves to coming forward and helping. The girl's manager was being as cagey as he could without implicating himself. It pained him to think it, but he was sure he had seen the young lad Brad look quite cheerful at one point. The aspiring actors and models he had questioned were all scared to involve themselves too much – their future careers at the front of their mind before the parents in Glasgow that were left without a daughter. There was an older gent who had seemed to upset to offer anything comprehensible, and on the other hand a handful of industry figures who seemed more upset at their cash cow no longer being around. The tabloid journalist had done absolutely nothing to negate the reputation of his profession.

There was one person on the island who seemed committed to finding Ava's killer, other than the police themselves. From the moment Murphy had held onto him on the beach, feeling his muscles give up and his weight bringing him to his knees, he knew that Richard Dickson was consumed with the need for justice. He would be keeping an eye on him, just as Rankin had asked, but not because he thought he was the murderer - because he believed that he was the key to solving this thing. Wherever Richard was, he wouldn't let himself be too far away. He sipped his thermos and thought of Chloe once more, forcing them to be happy thoughts.

"This is the first time you've come to see me."
David was glad Tara was facing the other way as he approached, because she would've seen his reaction to her opening remarks otherwise. He forced a smile.

"I've not quite known what to say, T." Ava had called her that but when he said it, it sounded more like a dig. She turned around, wiping her eyes. He had never seen her look so gaunt. Despite the countless hours the pair had spent together, there was a silent agreement that they never really got to the stage of liking one another. In fact, David was quietly pleased that soon he wouldn't have to see her ever again. He knew Tara would feel the same deep down, he had just realised it quicker.

"How's the kid?" David asked, as begrudgingly as ever.

"Brad? He seems okay. Not like you to ask about him."

"Never really knew how to approach the whole children thing. Not my bag." David said.

The two of them locked eyes in silence, years of bitterness threatening to finally come to the surface. What was the point now? Tara thought. They had held it together this long.

"Who killed her David?"

"I don't appreciate your tone, Tara."

"Well it is what it is. The two of us knew her better than anybody here. My drink was spiked – I barely saw her all night and even if I did I wouldn't remember it. That leaves you. You who's been avoiding me ever since." Tara said.

"Don't flatter yourself. Neither of us ever wanted to speak on the good days let alone now."

"Still, you're not wondering what she was like all day before she died? You were weirdly distant for someone who hasn't taken his eyes off her for her entire career." Her tone was an accusing one, and he wasn't taking kindly to id.

"I had things to do." David replied.

"Oh I know all about what you get up to. Ava told me everything."

David processed for a second before tightening his posture.

"Well that makes two of us. I guess that's what one might call a deadlock."

"Who killed her?" Tara stood up and raised her voice.

"Are you accusing me? If you are, I'd rather you just come out and say it."

The words were on the tip of her tongue, but his *deadlock* comment rang in her ears and stopped her from speaking. He was right. He knew things about Ava and Tara that she prayed would never be spoken. The fact that that would remain the case until one of them died themselves made her want to cry tears she didn't have left.

"Anyway." He said, picking up some of Ava's jewelry from the table. "I think you should be asking that question closer to home."

"Don't you dare."

"That little Satanist shit next door has trouble written all over his face."

"Stop it." Tara moved towards him, acting on instinct.

"Bad idea." He said, barely looking at her advancing figure. He was right though, and she halted.

"Brad's innocent in all of this."

David's silence was response enough. The threat was as clear as the view out to the water – *keep your mouth shut and I'll do the same.*

"Get out." She said, raising a finger towards the door but struggling to hide it shaking. He looked to be considering it before turning.

"It's been a hell of a ride." David shut the door behind him, leaving Tara with a mess of thoughts and sadness. They quickly turned to anger as she heard David exit the front door. He embodied everything she hated about men. Caring for nobody but himself, willing to drown anybody to keep his head above water. Could he have killed Ava? She had no doubt in her mind. She had overheard him spouting his alibi to anybody who would listen. The ladies he was with all night, what they discussed, the time it took. Tara was certain that it would be backed up, all by people like her - people he had a hold over. She turned the lock on the door even though she had watched him walk away from the house. The sound of the mechanism brought her back to the night Ava died. In her drunken and drugged state it had taken countless attempts to get the door locked. Why had she not given up and collapsed on the bed?

Like a flood it came back to her. Brad. They had argued like never before. He had been screaming at her. She was terrified, so locking the door seemed necessary. She retraced her steps, even adding in a stumble for the performance. The bass from the party had been making her head spin and as soon as she lay down – because she hadn't the strength to stay sitting up – she felt like she could be sick. Brad storming back downstairs had caused her to focus and the sickness to replaced again by fear. She had known he went back outside – the detectives had been quick to tell her – but where? He said it was to clear his head, but had he ever did that before? No, he was more the hide under the covers type. She remembered now crawling to the window and hoisting herself up to look out. If she had had the strength, she would've followed him. Again with the reenactment, she knelt on the floor and pulled herself up by the window sill so her eyes were just high enough to see outside. When she blinked slowly, the view of the party came back to her. If it was all a construct of her mind, she would never know – but it seemed more like memory than fantasy. Now, with her eyes fully shut, she searched the scene for Brad. It only took a moment until she remembered him stomping through the party and towards the campsite. The campsite, of course, was in between the party and the cliffs. She fell backwards and hit the wooden floor with a thump, just as she had that night.

25

Complete darkness. The house, the portable lights of the campsite and the moonlight all became distant behind him as he neared the castle ruins. Tomorrow, his life would change paths dramatically once again. The suicidal thoughts weren't quite showing themselves but teasing the fact that they may soon. As he got closer to the old castle, the shine of two quad bikes sent Richard's heart racing. He didn't know why, but the tension in his muscles told him to enter survival mode. Creeping behind the one wall that remained fully intact, he pressed himself close to the cold stone and kept moving. Quickly, the grass beneath his feet turned to rubble. The conversation inside was hushed – too quiet for him to pick up any parts of it. One thing was for certain, it wasn't small talk. The two voices spoke short sentences in between long silences as the wind whistled through the architectural shell. No movement or exploration either. They were standing still. A serious, and secret, meeting. Richard's foot slipped down into a ditch about half a metre deep.

His hands met the ground before he fell completely, and he held himself in position like a gymnast while the noise of some stones falling subsided. It seemed like the loudest thing in the world. The voices stopped for a second. Footsteps. They were coming towards him. Richard sidled closer into the wall, well aware of the tall and narrow window space not far from him. The footsteps stopped beside it – they were assertive, almost exaggerated. One of them was at the window on the inside now. All they had to do was lean out and Richard would be spotted like a fox in the bushes. The person didn't move, and no head nor hand breached the window. He could hear husky, deep breaths. Definitely those of a man. He'd have to exhale soon himself - the tension on his temple was becoming unbearable. The sharp stones started to breach the skin on his palms and his foot was starting to cramp, but one movement and he'd be caught. The second voice – the one further away – said something again. It was a desperate whisper. The man whose breath Richard was close enough to hear finally turned away. He took the same footsteps as before, the soles of his shoes clapping the hard ground like a horse on concrete.

A strong gust of wind gave Richard the opportunity to breath and move. He did, crawling underneath the window and towards the cliffs. He looked out to where the boat had stopped earlier. The ocean looked like oil, dark and thick. It sloshed onto the rocks below as he made his way down a small drop. There was another window above him, and the wall had been partly torn down by the elements. He crouched on the smashed stone and leant his back as straight against the wall as much it would allow. The voices were at it again, faster this time, but every word uttered still seemed considered and vital. Both men. Both tense, almost angry. If he could just stand, a moment of silence from the wind and water might let him identify them. A slight shuffle of his feet caused some rubble to crackle, and he knew that to move would be to be found. He gripped his chest with his hand, hoping to silence his thumping heart. The conversation was slowing again, this time for good it seemed. Richard looked out into the darkness. He urged himself to fall. There would be no guilt about leaving his Dad, or Mary's memory. It would be an accident. If he happened to clear the sharp rocks directly below, the water would take care of him. No boats, no beach – nobody would know until tomorrow. *Fall* he told himself. *Do it. Lose your balance.* Ava's memory returned, pushing everything else out of his head. She didn't fall or lose her balance. She was strangled, beaten and dropped. Just like Mary had been before her. They both called on him for help – help that he couldn't provide. Twice in his life now he had the chance to stand and be counted, and what had he done? Cried and not shown up. But when De Rossi's story went live in the morning, he didn't want to be around for it. *You're slipping.* He told himself. *Let it happen.* His back arched from the wall and his head weighed his frame forward. *Not long to go now.* Richard's arms, as if out of his control, left the safety of the terrain and stretched out. His body rocked forwards and back, forwards and back. *Do it.* The wind was on the side of death as well, finding a way behind him and urging him towards the cold, dark depths below. *Just a bit further.* Suddenly, an engine roared. Then another. Just like that, his balance was solid. The quadbikes burst off into the distance. To Richard, it was identical to the sound of the van taking Mary away. But this time, he could do something about it.

He scrambled up to the higher ground, feeling the wind failing to knock him back down. No sign of the two men. He cursed himself for not being able to recognise even one of the voices as he entered the castle. No physical sign had been left behind, but the smell hit his nostrils as he inhaled deeply. Aftershave, and not a particularly nice one. He remembered considering making a petty insult to De Rossi earlier at the beach about his choice of scent. It smelled even worse now, lingering in the air like a toxic gas. De Rossi, a murderer? Maybe, but he couldn't be sure until he could identify the man he was arguing with in this very space. His *editor*, he thought. He closed his eyes tightly, not that it made things much darker. Confident footsteps, heavy breath, an angry tone. Who was he? The answer seemed further away the more he thought about it – everybody had acted with a filter, so he had seen no tempers or anger. What that told him was that while Ava's death may not have been planned, the killer was a master at keeping his cool. An altogether more sinister person than first thought. It hadn't been a drunken fight or a push and a tumble.

Richard's eyes opened as an engine came into earshot once again. This time, it was coming towards him. He cursed the sound that was quickly becoming a trigger for danger. The quad bike arrived outside and went silent. Nowhere to hide now. He grabbed a stone – small enough to fit in his palm but heavy enough to do some damage should it be required. He held it tight behind his back. The click-clack of footsteps grew louder. Were they the same as before? Almost impossible to tell.

"Fucking hell!" Brad's voice switched from low to high and then back again. Could it be an act? It was pretty good if so. Richard's hand eased around the stone slightly, letting the blood circulate again.

"Forget something?" He said.

"What? I've never been here before." Brad said, as suspicious of Richard as he was of him.

"Must've been someone else." Richard said, leaning his lower back against the bottom of the window. He fancied his chances against the teenager if it came to it.

"Did you walk here? Are you on your own?" Brad asked, edging ever so slightly into the ruins. Richard decided to let go of the stone, attempting to place it on the ledge behind him. It clattered out and down towards the water. He ignored it, hoping Brad would too.

"Yeah, I wanted to clear my head." The headache pounded once as a stark reminder. "What are you doing out here?"

In response, Brad kicked a stone. "Same, I guess." He said.

"You finding it tough?"

If Richard had to draw a troubled teen, it wouldn't look far off Brad. His head arched forward so when he looked at you it was always under arched eyebrows that created a menacing shadow. His long, dark fringe was constantly gravitating to the middle of his forehead, swept back with a limp wrist every so often. His jeans were tight and t-shirt was baggy, highlighting a gangling, almost skeletal, frame.

"They think I did it." Brad said, immediately looking at Richard for a reaction.

"Why do you think that?"

"I could tell. Plus, I was outside when it happened."

"Were you alone?" Richard asked.

Brad nodded, and Richard weighed up the chances that he was standing across from a murderer. The motive wasn't hard to find – it would be easy to argue that Ava had prevented a normal childhood for him. She had commanded Tara's attention, the attention which, as a mother, should have been focused on her child.

"I heard you had a bit of an argument with your mum." Richard said. One benefit of the island was that not much stayed secret for long. The people there made their money from gossip, speculation and reactions.

"It wasn't really an argument. She could barely speak."

"You know her drink was spiked, right?"

Brad nodded again, moving around the ruins now and taking in whatever little detail that the darkness was allowing.

"And you gave her a drink at one point, didn't you?" Richard continued.

Brad stopped exploring at that.

"So?" His voice had a hint of an unpredictable anger within. Richard found himself regretting dropping the stone.

"If you don't want to tell me that's fine, but you better have a good answer when the police ask you."

"You think I'd drug my own mum?"

"All I'm saying is that it's not a good look."

"She'd had plenty before then. Could've been another drink."

"Could've been." Richard agreed, but not really.

"It was your friend who asked me to give her it, anyway. Said she had asked for it."

"What friend?" For the first time, Richard moved closer to him. This was the second tense exchange of the night that the castle walls were privy to. He wondered how many more had taken place over the years. It seemed a fitting location – almost as if it drew the confrontation in like a magnet.

"The other journalist – the one who was always writing about Ava." Brad said.

De Rossi. Wherever Richard searched, his name popped up.

136

"Paul De Rossi gave you a drink and asked you to give it to Tara?" Richard watched Brad nod. "And did you tell the police?"

"No, not yet."

"Brad, you have to tell them things like this. It might be the difference between you having a life or spending your best years in jail."

"You think he had something to do with Ava's murder?" Brad asked. Richard sensed that the young man had thought about little else than himself today, and was just now becoming as intrigued and horrified as he should've been all along.

"I don't know, but like I said –"

"-It's not a good look." Brad nodded.

"So why don't you want to tell the police where you went at the end of the night?"

"It's none of their business. Or yours."

"Can you see why that might not get you off the hook?" Richard wanted to shake him.

"I saw you."

The atmosphere dropped and what little heat was within the ruins seemed to disappear.

"What do you mean by that?" Richard asked slowly, buying himself time for what could be coming. *What could be coming?*

"In your tent. With that girl."

"What girl?"

"I don't know. Some girl. You don't even know, do you?" Brad's tone was judgemental.

"That's none of your business, Brad. And if I were you I'd be worried about spying on people when they're – you know – having a private moment."

"And what if she gets pregnant? What will you do then?"

Richard couldn't quite believe what he was hearing. He was being lectured by a teenage boy. More irritating still was that it reminded of something he would've come out with at that age.

"Where did you go after that?" He pushed on, becoming more suspicious by the second.

Brad turned his back now, looking up towards the night sky

through the large gaps in the caved- in roof.

"It's stupid." He said.

"Well then nobody will think you're lying." Richard said, stepping closer to him a bit more.

"My mum couldn't put two words together when I was helping her to bed, but she did manage to tell me something." Brad turned back around, sensing Richard's presence. The two were standing a bit too close for comfort now, but neither moved. "She was crying and shaking, pushing me away from her." He lifted a sleeve and showed Richard some raw scratch marks. "Then when she was finally in bed I turned the light off and was ready to leave, when she told me that -" Some tears were streaming down Brad's face now. He didn't bother hiding it. "- she told me that my dad was here."

26

The tears had continued as Brad recounted his life story to Richard within the wrecked castle. Cynically, he had started off not feeling very sorry for the teenager. He had travelled the world, wanted for nothing and would probably be set for life. Poor boy. But then he remembered that pain and sadness were relative – who was he to judge? The hole that had been left from never knowing his father was clearly something that affected his life every day. Richard got the sense that in Brad's mind, the man took one look at him as a baby and decided that he wasn't worth the effort. It would be hard to convince him otherwise, even though the much more likely scenario was a one-night stand and Tara deciding to go it alone.

At one point during the exchange, he was certain Brad was going to ask him if he was his dad. He was glad he didn't, because he would've struggled to hide his sympathy for the boy. It was quite clear that Brad did not want sympathy, however much he deserved it. Still, he was damaged. That was unquestionable. What's worse, was he placed part of the blame on Ava. *She made us go everywhere with her.* He had sneered. The seventeen-year-old had a grudge against celebrities in general. Richard had taken a step back when he had broken into a venomous rant about influencer culture and social media, bursting like a bottle that had been shaken up for the last two days. *What do they do except make us all feel bad about ourselves?* He had asked, seething. Richard was inclined to agree. Unlike Brad, who was baptized in the fire, he had watched the flames of social media spark, flicker and spread. It often worried him – the sense of power it gave the powerless, the possibility of anonymity, the exposure to too much too often. Of course, there were positives, but every day they seemed to be popping under the pressure of the negatives. In his admittedly pessimistic mind, Richard could see a pandemic of suicide coming the likes of nothing anybody had ever seen before. Brad, he thought, could quite easily be a statistic in all of that. Still, since his sister was killed as a child he had known that predicting what would happen tomorrow was a waste of time. Knowing that what was to come could be unimaginable was the main source of his poorly managed anxiety.

He lay back in his tent, feeling every bump and dip in the ground beneath him. Had Ava ever felt nervous? Or scared? He knew she must've, but her being so good at hiding it made it hard to predict when it happened. On quiet nights like this one, when she was alone in bed, what stopped her from sleeping? The arguments with Tara? The fear of ending up alone? The people who were desperate to see her fall from grace? Looking around the island you'd be forgiven for thinking that everybody in the industry wanted her to succeed. That was the big problem with finding the killer – one had to look amongst people who faked it for a living. A seemingly perfect crime under the noses of the law and some of the biggest gossip columnists the country had to offer. He ran through the list of the people he suspected the most for the hundredth time as if they were the only ones in his life. Nothing new came to mind, so he switched to finding a motive. Love? Maybe. Money? Maybe. De Rossi mentioned that she was making a big career change, stepping out of the spotlight. Richard had heard whisperings of it across the island before her death – so much so that it seemed some were here for the announcement rather than the celebration. Who would a career change hurt the most? David and Tara. Brad as well, but he probably wouldn't see it that way. If that allegation against her two closest colleagues wasn't flimsy enough, Richard couldn't help but argue that they would probably be okay without Ava. Tara might even welcome a break, and David was quite clearly a survivor. He thought back to their schooldays and that fleeting romance. Ava would hold onto information for the longest time, bringing up past mistakes and grievances like they had happened seconds before. If Richard had looked at another girl as they walked into a party, she'd use it as ammo a year later. He hated it, but was silently impressed at her ability to not react in the moment. If revenge should be served cold, she was plating it up with mould and flies surrounding it.

Maybe one day you'll tell my story she had said, only hours before it had been brought to an end. Strange for someone who lived their life so openly to think they still had a story to tell, unless there was something that had been kept hidden. She was ready to change that, only Richard couldn't see it until now and it was too late. So she wanted to right a wrong, and maybe the person it involved stopped her in the harshest way. Richard dug his nails into the tent and tried to separate a chunk of ground from the island. Every time he settled on something in the investigation, more questions rained down. Finding the feud that led to Ava's death was hard considering the celebrity world had more of them than stiletto heels. Pointing to a murderer amongst the 200 people was like finding the rock on the beach that was used to knock Ava unconscious. As he heard a wave crash, he admitted to himself that he was out of his depth. Some laughter from a distance away was his lifeboat, so he moved towards it.

"Can we talk?" Richard said. The fire's flames danced off the lenses of Devin's sunglasses. He was hosting a group of people, drinking and laughing tentatively. If he hadn't remembered Richard before, the mutterings of suspicion had sorted that.

"Hey, of course." He said, with a cheery enough tone to show that if he wasn't on his side, he also wasn't on the against him either. The others around the campfire made no attempt to not stare at Richard. He turned and walked away and Devin followed. His shorts were hiked up showing toned and tanned thighs, and he had retired every button but one on the Hawaiian shirt.

"Bit late for you isn't it?" He said to Richard.

"Couldn't sleep. Doesn't it feel strange having a good time given what's happened?"

"Not once you're doing it. I loved Ava, but a guy's got to live." Devin replied. The pair sat down on some chairs that had been there since the party. Behind them, a clearing led back to the house and the campsite. It was here they first spoke, and the first time Richard came face to face with David.

"It's funny, I've heard that a lot." Richard said.

"Heard what?"

"How people here loved her. Not everybody can be telling the truth."

"I meant love as in *love your shoes*." Having said it, Devin looked down at Richard's bare feet. He grinned. "You get what I mean."

"What I'm trying to figure out is who didn't love her. Who hated her? Who was scared of her?" Richard asked.

"Scared of her?"

"Or of what she would do."

Devin sat back and took two cigarettes from a pack in his shirt pocket. Richard accepted the offer of one. They lit up in silence and exhaled, watching the smoke meet in the air between them.

"Why?" Devin asked.

"What did you know about an announcement she was going to make? Any truth to it?"

"Almost certainly. What it was though? I know as much as everybody else." Devin made a zero with his fingers and blew a ribbon of smoke through it.

"Suppose it was about someone else and not herself. Who did she have that info on?"

"Hard to say. You really think it was her style to put someone on the spot like that?"

"It depends what they did, doesn't it?" Richard said.

"Well then you should speak to your fellow journo. Nobody rode her coattails like he did."

Richard was reminded of the story that would be posted online by the morning. It was all the more reason to get information tonight when people would still risk being seen with him.

"What do you think of David?"

Devin coughed a bit.

"As in did he kill her?" He said.

"Yeah."

"I don't see why he would choose here and now."

One of the ladies by the fire shouted Devin and told him that they were turning in.

"Better go." He said to Richard, happy with the distraction. Richard watched him walk off. In a matter of seconds, he was completely alone and telling himself to not let any fear in. The fire was fighting to stay lit, and would be for hours. It would lose its battle before sunrise. He inhaled deeply and wondered why Devin had questioned the timing rather than the motive.

DAY 3

27

HART-LESS: Inside the superstar murder investigation. EXCLU-SIVE. By Paul De Rossi.

Richard had to admire De Rossi's work. Even if he hadn't been involved, this story was not something he would scroll by. The picture of Ava was one from taken at the launch of her channel and app. He had seen it before – her smile was one of pure joy, as if the camera on the red carpet was an old friend she hadn't seen for years. The kind of happiness that was hard to fake. And yet, Richard noticed the same hint of emptiness in her eyes that he had seen more and more in his research into her career. For the woman who simply had everything, life still wasn't that simple. Or could it be hindsight playing tricks? Alongside Ava, there was a picture of the island, shot from beneath and in low light to give it an extra menacing vibe. Richard turned on his side, back cracking and feet cold, to continue reading the story that would dictate the direction in which his life was about to go in. It was 5AM on Sunday.

The investigation into STARLET SENSATION Ava Hart's brutal mystery killing continued on Saturday. Detectives are interviewing everyone who is currently camping on what's being called MURDER ISLAND by some of the shaken guests, who we can reveal are not leaving for fear of being labelled the killer.

Miss Hart, 35, was brutally strangled, beaten and thrown over a cliff edge on the first night of a celebrity getaway to celebrate her birthday. The lavish party on an unoccupied island off the coast of

Scotland was seen as strange by some, as Ava was known to prefer smaller affairs with her inner circle. Yesterday, we revealed that she had been thought to have spent six figures on the celebration that saw friends and foes from the industry invited. In one of the strangest crimes in a long time, one that belongs in a Hollywood movie, there is a murderer on the guestlist. So far, no one has come forward with any information that will help the police's investigation, which is now under increasing pressure from top brass.

Among the stranded guests is Hayley Dee, who was once a fierce rival of Ava's, but told us of her heartbreak over the murder. "Ava and I were constantly competing, but we both needed that to push us further forward in our careers. Nobody deserves to be taken so young and in their prime. I'm honoured to say that before her death we cleared the air. I'm just so sad that we'll never see what a partnership would have looked like. She was amazing at what she did and had incredible plans not just for her career, but to help those less fortunate. I'll carry her memory forward with me forever."

As the hours stack up, the police's interviews seem to be following certain lines of enquiry that they hope will lead them to Hart's killer. One guest, who asked to remain nameless, told us that they were unimpressed by the investigation. "How hard can it be? A woman is dead and we're all stuck here like criminals until they work out who the killer is. Some people are already discussing leaving. At this point, it's a human rights issue. I've not had a shower in 24 hours. We're all having to share phone chargers. I feel for Ava's fans and her family, but they need to let the innocent people leave."

Ava Hart shot to fame in her late teens after being talent scouted at her Glasgow high school. She fronted popular children's show "Play House" before a short spell out of the limelight for mental health reasons. Upon her return, her rise through the echelons of celebrity continued, often commanding presenting roles on prime time shows. Ava segued into modelling and her own line of cosmetics before successfully launching her own app and online channel, called

A.V.A. Her untimely death has cut her life and career short, with many left wondering what further heights she would have reached had she not been brutalised and killed at her own birthday party that only a select number of guests were invited to. Despite this, the police seem to be scratching their heads.

SHOWBIZ BIG-WIG Herbert Hargreaves was in attendance to celebrate with Ava almost 20 years after discovering her. He told us that whoever was responsible should own up and that the industry as a whole needed to change for the better. "The pressure put on young stars these days is incredible, even more so as they struggle to keep any parts of their lives out of the public eye. I'm not sure if it was jealousy, a career-feud or something else entirely, but the murderer should be caught and face the full force of the law." When prompted to speculate on the suspects, Hargreaves refused, only going as far as to say: "There are certainly a few people that the police should be looking at more closely."

Amongst those in attendance is DISGRACED JOURNALIST Richard Dickson, currently reeling from a scandalous story in which he accused politician Gareth Young of sexual assault. The claims have since been found to be baseless and false. We can exclusively reveal that before his failed career in the media, he pursued Ava as a love interest as a teen. It is understood that he was incensed when she left their local area in search of fame, cutting ties with him altogether. We reached out to Young for comment. He told us that he would not interfere in a murder enquiry that he knew little about, and was confident that the police would identify and arrest the guilty party. He also expressed his sorrow for Hart's parents, who both survive her. Finally, he refused to comment on the allegations made by Richard Dickson, rightly referring to them as "inappropriate" and "a backwards step in the very real battle against sexual assault in our communities." Dickson, who remains on the island and is being questioned intensely by the police, refused to comment. Hart's team have refused to answer questions about whether or not he was invited in the first place, or simply turned up to satisfy his alleged ob-

session with the superstar.

Meanwhile, Ava Hart's empire carries on. Views on her past videos have shot up by millions and been flooded with comments of condolence and heartbreak. A company representative told us that subscriber numbers had increased five-fold. Whispers about who will replace her as the nation's premiere influencer have made their way around the industry, with many citing Hayley as the rightful heir. In a classy response, Hayley has cancelled all of her upcoming engagements and removed all of her social media posts other than a tribute to Ava and her groundbreaking work.

Rumours that Hart was readying an announcement for a new venture can't be confirmed, but one thing is for sure – whatever she was planning next has been cruelly taken from her fans. As a celebrity with incredible influence, it was thought that Hart would begin to use that to help others less fortunate. In her last interview with this paper, she expressed a desire to change society for the better. "As we get older, I think we begin to reflect not only on our own lives but how they compare to others. I've been blessed, but I've had my fair share of troubles, and I see similar things happening to people all over the world everyday. Whatever comes next, my focus will be on giving those people a voice." Ava Hart, only just 35, will be remembered as much for her stunningly good looks as her ambition and drive – an example to young girls everywhere.

Investigating officers refused to contribute to our story, citing the ongoing investigation and respect for the deceased as a reason to keep certain details private. Thoughts from the guests on the island, however, take a different view of why they refused to comment.

"It's embarrassing for the police to have no solid suspects after 24 hours. Meanwhile Ava's parents are heartbroken, her fans are in mourning and we're stuck here with a cold-blooded killer."

It would seem that much will happen over the next 24 hours, and there is a sincere hope on MURDER ISLAND that the killer will be identified and arrested. In the meantime, the guests look set to stay put, with the fear of seeming guilty by leaving too great. Most are quietly keeping to themselves and updating their families on their wellbeing. Others, however, are already despicably capitalising on Miss Hart's murder – using it to grow followers or deflect from other DISGRACEFUL scandals they may be involved in. The sad fact that some would seek to gain from such a tragedy paints a very stark picture of celebrity culture and our society in general…

For live, uninterrupted, 24/7 coverage and updates on the investigation, visit our blog.

Richard squeezed his phone, willing it to break into pieces. He wondered how few people would see the irony in the act of capitalising on death whilst shaming others for doing just the same. With a second glance, he noted the stark absence of David and Tara. Tara, he assumed, would've rightly slammed the door in De Rossi's face when asked for comment, but David was a different story entirely. He thrived off of attention and an opportunity to act the endearing manager was one Richard was sure he would capitalise on… Unless he wanted his name as far away from the investigation as possible. Unless he was the one nudging the finger of guilt towards Richard.

In terms of damage inflicted to him, it was catastrophic. De Rossi, unlike when he was dressing himself, was a master of subtle placement and creating a very convincing picture. Any mention of Richard was framed by negativity and slander that wasn't quite sue-able. The same nouns were used when discussing him and the murderer. A picture, one from the party that he hadn't yet seen, was used to break up the copy. In it, his face was bruised and mid-speak, giving him a psychotic look that he couldn't quite believe wasn't digitally altered. One positive – nay the only positive – was that he could finally identify whom he had spent the night with, because she was draped over him in the picture.

28

The guests moved away from Richard as he made his way through the crowd, avoiding the space like there was a force surrounding him. The De Rossi effect. Looking at the positives, it helped him identify who he was looking for. It didn't take long to spot the shock of orange hair - Emily was clearly in need of a proper shower.

"Can we talk?" Richard asked as her two right hand ladies moved shoulder to shoulder with her for protection, just like the had on the train when they first met.

"It's okay." Emily told them. She nodded in the direction of the horizon and expected Richard to follow her as she walked towards it. He did. The sun was still heating up – readying itself to dry the dew on the grass. There were no clouds to stop it.

"You bastard." Emily raised her hand and Richard instinctively covered his already messed up face. Instead, she went to his stomach, making a fist on the way down and giving him a worthy shot in the gut. Her arched eyebrows and cartoonish scowl brought some memories back, and Richard felt a hint of the attraction that he had followed through with the night of the party. There could be a few things that made him deserve the punch. Was it because he hadn't spoken to her until now? Had he upset her that night? Could be that he was suspected of murder? Probably the latter.

"Look, I'm sorry. For anything and everything. And thanks for speaking to me just now – it's probably not a great look for you." Emily shrugged as if she could care less what the other guests thought at this point. "You don't think I did it, do you?" He asked, naively.

"Honey, if you were too drunk to *you know*, then you were too drunk to murder someone. I know you didn't do it."

So no sex – that was probably good, all things considered. He thought back to a similar night towards the end of high school with Ava. Both too drunk to remember what had happened, and too embarrassed to admit that. It was one of the last nights they spent together.

"I can't remember a thing – I really hope I wasn't an idiot."

"You lied to me." Emily said, pouting as she would in a selfie.

"Did I? What about?"

"You let me call you my fucking *prince* all night." Her words ended in a whisper. Richard, like most of the trip, was lost.

"Sorry, what is it you mean?" Emily dragged his arm, moving him in closer to her.

"I thought - " She looked over his shoulder to make sure nobody was around. " - somebody told me you were, y'know, royalty."

"Excuse me?"

"Someone fucking told me you were a part of the fucking Royal family you fuck!" She said it through her teeth, her cheeks reddening with embarrassment rather than anger.

Richard started to laugh, and it felt like he wasn't going to stop anytime soon. It felt good. For the past couple of months, he had soaked up pain like rain in the dirt. To let laughter come to the surface was a small miracle. He went to speak but no, he still couldn't stop his hysterics. Emily had tried to bag a Windsor and had ended up with a wanker. She wanted a Duke and found a dick. He had been convulsing so long now that she could only smile. "Stop it." She said through the grin. "Seriously. Stop it."

"You met me on the train, surely you knew then that the only thing I was heir to was male pattern baldness?"

"I thought you might have been doing an undercover thing. Anyway it was someone at the party who told me."

"Who?" Richard asked, sensing something more sinister at play. The island seemed to bring it out of people.

"I can't remember. Anyway, please can we just never talk

about this again thank you." Emily's American accent had a satisfying rhythm to it. Richard decided against asking just how far things went before he passed out, sparing her any further blushes. Finally over his hysteria and firmly back on the island, he got down to business.

"You have to tell the police that we were together."

"Ew, no." Emily said, checking her nails. Again, subjectively it was funny just how little she valued him. He would've laughed once more if he didn't potentially face life in jail.

"Emily." He finally remembered her name. "It's a murder investigation. I'm not asking you to shout it from the rooftops, just tell the detectives."

"Fine. But this stays between us after that."

"No second date?" Richard said. Emily looked to be genuinely considering it before scoffing at him.

"Not going well for you, is it?" She said.

"No, you're right. If the press don't lay off I'll call the Queen and ask for a favour."

They each let a smile slip through, silently agreeing a truce. As she moved away, Richard remembered one last thing.

"You brought me a drink didn't you?"

"So?" she said.

"Did you get it from the bar?"

"No, some guy asked me to give it to you."

"Who?"

"Fat guy. Looked Italian." She shrugged and made her way towards the crowd. All eyes were on Richard. De Rossi was nowhere to be seen.

DI Rankin was struggling to contain his rage. Along with DS Donnelly, he had arrived back on the island that morning, having spent a frustrating hour with Ava's parents the night before. Every now and then he felt his knee jerk under the table, or a muscle in his foot twitch. Everything up top had to remain calm and stay still. What he wanted to do was grab the journalist's oversized collar and rattle him off the walls like he was shaking sand from a towel at the beach. He knew better though. The snake would claim harassment in a heartbeat. Over the years, Rankin had found that it was impossible to win against a certain type of person. Paul De Rossi was that type. The story - which he had had to read twice because his tremors made him miss parts – was more than insulting, it was dangerous. DS Donnelly had shared his anger, but she did so in the way that women tended to – much more practically. Still, her sharp expression said enough. They were going to do what they could to make life hell for De Rossi. Once they were done with that dressing down, Brad was next on the hit list to discuss what they had found on his phone which was interesting to say the least. Incriminating? Rankin was yet to decide.

"These sources – care to name any of them?" He asked De Rossi. His first question after minutes of silent tension. He wanted to be waving a rolled-up newspaper, but one hadn't reached the island. Instead, he was tapping his phone like he was playing candy crush. It didn't have the same effect.

"You know I can't do that, Detective." De Rossi sat with a forced posture, recognising this as a moment in which professionalism was key. The paper's lawyers would take care of anything the police took umbrage with.

"You've got your place on the food chain, De Rossi – I won't argue against that. But when the lions come to town the dung beetles get out of the way." Rankin wasn't laughing, which made it funnier. De Rossi tried hard to remain serious and succeeded, DS Donnelly did the same, although she struggled too. Her boss was a good detective, but a woeful trash talker. She was sure that if they ever had to attend a crime within a supermarket, he'd be the first to utter *clean up on aisle five* or something along those lines. Still, she was on his side, and had to back him up no matter how ridiculous he sounded. She thought she should break the silence brought on by his bizarre analogy, so she did.

"Richard Dickson."

"What about him?" De Rossi said.

"Come on – Stevie Wonder could see that you were trying to

put the blame on him. Why? Professional jealousy?"

"Not a bit of it." De Rossi scoffed, but it was clearly true on some level. "Anyway, just some observations, readers can make of it what they will."

"So why him?" She pressed.

"Why not? He's as much a suspect as anybody else at this point."

"You're telling me that you shut your eyes and went with who your finger landed on?"

"Well, no, but – "

"But what? You actually do have a reason to suspect him, and that means that you've been withholding information from us?" Donnelly summed it up nicely.

Rankin glanced proudly at his protégé. No matter how high she rose through the ranks, he could always take a little bit of credit.

"DS Donnelly is right – either you've falsely accused someone, or you've not been honest with us. Take your time now."

De Rossi remained as calm as he could, but he felt the sweat beginning to pool in the various creases of his body. He had played this over in his head since sending the story off for proofing. Telling them that more than one person had expressed an interest in seeing pressure put on Richard was, although true, out of the question. He wanted to distance himself from all of this – to be an outsider, someone whose part played wasn't even worth considering. In reality, that was far from the truth. Paul De Rossi had been created in the shadow of Ava Hart, and she had been a constant source of life for him. The fact that this sustenance was coming to an end had begun to worry him, and create a deep jealousy inside. Tara was commanding her attention and advising her to not speak to the press. At the same time, Ava was becoming self-sufficient. She had little reason to turn to the press for exposure nowadays and doing so could be more trouble than it was worth. He always knew that one day she would want to be in control, and it was clear that that day would have been today if she had lived to see it.

And then, the final straw – she had invited Richard. De Rossi had taken it as an open message that she would no longer be feeding him interviews and information to satisfy his hungry career. Even worse, the idiot didn't even seem to know that that was why he was on the island. He had come to realise that there was nothing so simultaneously important and fickle as a source. The secrets he had kept for her over the years, the way he had spun stories in her favour – had she forgotten all about that? No, dropping him at this point wouldn't do. If he couldn't have Ava, nobody could. Now, that turned out to be exactly the case. His one regret was that he couldn't get that final interview he had planned, after she had had a few drinks at the party, loose lipped and nostalgic. He was certain he could pick some details that would have made it front page worthy. Oh he did try – he tried hard, but in the end it wasn't to be. Oh well, save it for the book, he thought. That brought him back to Richard Dickson, who would undoubtedly be having the same thought just now. So yes, while he was influenced on the outside to put his fellow journalist in the frame, all that had served to do was give him the bright idea. Internally, he could admit that Dickson was the more talented of the two of them. Simple maths said that that wouldn't be the case if he was locked up for murder, or even considered for long enough to sweep the legs from his already shaky reputation. Survival – that's all this was. Something Paul De Rossi had become an expert at when everybody around him in the industry was dying off.

"No comment." He told the detectives. It wasn't pretty, but the dung beetle would live to fight another day.

29

Tara hated being selfish. It was something her mother had tried to drill out of her as a child, and had succeeded to an extent. Every now and then, she would feel it rising within her like scum in a blocked sink. It had happened that very morning. She, like everyone else, had read the story essentially accusing Richard of Ava's murder. Instead of worrying for the man who clearly meant a lot to her friend, she felt relieved that the police might overlook Brad. It wasn't noble or something she could admit, but it was how she felt. When she had finished the story that morning, she had considered letting it play out – saving Brad and watching Richard take the fall. Thankfully, her latest inspection of Ava's journal gave her something that may just help them both. She had found the source of Ava's tears. Her resentment. Her anger. Or at least she thought she had.

"How's the sickness?" Richard asked, finding her first even though she had been looking for him. They were standing in the kitchen of the house.

"It's been about 4 hours since last vomiting."

"You should have one of those signs like they have for accidents in the workplace." They smiled together, although it was tired and brief.

"There's something I want to show you. Will you come with me?" Tara said.

"Sure." The officers that were moving around the house cursed silently that their eavesdropping was over with. Tara and Richard climbed the stairs and entered her room.

"Are you okay?"

"I'm fine. Did you read it?" Richard asked. Of course she had.

Tara nodded, unsure of what to say.

"And?" He pushed for a response.

"And I still don't think you had anything to do with it."

Richard mouthed the words thank you, fearing that if he spoke them his voice would faulter. It was the first kindness he had felt from someone since he last spoke with Ava. Tara unlocked a drawer beside the bed and took out a tablet. He was suitably intrigued.

"Ava's?"

"Mine, but with access to her cloud drive." She answered as she tapped in a passcode that was at least eight digits long. Richard's was his birthday.

"I was reminiscing a bit. She wrote a sort-of diary for a ladies mag a while back. Seems like she enjoyed the idea of writing her thoughts down, and kept it going in private."

"A journal? I didn't think this could get any more *murder mystery*."

"You should be glad it does. I'm pretty sure it puts you in the clear."

No more daft jokes now - he had her full attention.

"See she gets quite introspective. It's sad really. There's never any mention of the incredible trips we took, the celeb gossip or the success. Her subject is her feelings – and she had a lot more negative ones than I ever knew about."

"Don't we all?"

"I suppose. So here." Tara zoomed in on the document that was hundreds of pages long, only separated by underlined dates here and there. "Sorry. Not there – here." She moved the location and shook her head at the fact that none of her organisational skills had rubbed off on Ava over the years. Richard caught quick glances of the content, which seemed more stream of consciousness than narrative.

"It took a while to hit me, but whenever she's talking about the dark side of the industry, there's always a reference to *him*."

"Who?" Richard asked.

"She's not made it that easy. It's *him* – that's the word she uses.

Everything that's bad in the world can somehow be compared to something he's done, or something she thinks he would do. It's like an obsession."

"Give me an example."

She scrolled and found a passage.

"Okay – like this." They both read.

Dad phoned today and reminded me in his own subtle way what a man should be – honourable and kind. Why are so few the same? I wish Dad was what I pictured when I closed my eyes and thought of humanity, but he's not. Instead, I can't get away from the image of him. A coward. A user. A poisonous presence. A fake. A fraud. A power trip personified. No, not simply a trip – a journey. What can I do? I made the power 100 list this year, and I've never felt so power-less. My greatest trick was convincing anybody else otherwise. And yet, more and more, I find myself asking what have I to lose? The stars will align soon.

"And you've no idea who it is?" Richard asked.

"I wouldn't say that. She says talks about him here when she's reminiscing about one of her first award shows – that tells me it's someone she's known for a long time."

"Which means David."

"Technically it could."

"You're not convinced he did it?"

"Trust me, it wouldn't take much to change my mind." Tara said.

"What about this bit – *the year I disappeared.* What does she mean by that?"

Tara's face lost some colour as she read over the passage he was referring to.

"It was the year she quit everything and went into hiding."

"Mental health struggles they said?" Richard asked.

Tara's index finger moved to her eyelid and made one stroke across. She didn't respond.

"Why haven't you given this to the police?"

Silence again.

"Tara, if you know something you need to tell me. They're probably a few hours away from arresting me. Why did she go off the grid?"

"She swore me to secrecy. It's the one thing I promised I would never say." Tara knew that it sounded pathetic in the grand scheme of things.

"And if it leads us to her killer?"

She thought about it for a second, and then a few more. After a minute, Richard reached out and held her shoulder.

"What if it leads us to *him?*" He repeated.

"It won't. It can't. It has nothing to do with that – it's -"

The door creaked open and DS Donnelly crossed the threshold, letting some of the tension out.

"Mr Dickson, could we have a word?"

Richard had known it was coming. He would get nothing more from Tara at that point, so stood up to go with the police.

"Please." He said to her. It had been coming for a long time now, but he began to feel complete deflation. Why was nobody stepping forward with information? Tara had some, and he was certain De Rossi and David did too. There were probably many others on top of that, and yet they would all rather let him take the fall than risk complicating their own lives or revealing their own secrets. He was truly beginning to understand the selfishness of celebrity, and it disgusted him.

Tara avoided all eye contact as he left, essentially being dragged along by DS Donnelly. Her and Ava's biggest secret couldn't be the key to all of this, could it? Or had she been blinded by love and loyalty? She heard the door shut behind Richard and swallowed deeply The selfishness had a way of burning her lungs, and right now they felt ablaze.

In a strange way, the party atmosphere was returning somewhat. After De Rossi's article, the hunt for Ava's killer seemed almost over, and it was a reason to celebrate. That, and the guests were mostly a part of the microwave generation – rarely did something consume them for an extended period of time. It seemed, as some had predicted, that they had never really been Ava's friends at all. David held court around a makeshift café that had been cobbled together with benches, hot water urns and unlabeled jars of instant coffee. Since the event staff had stopped working, the menial jobs had fallen to the guests with the lowest status in their world. Some of the more well-known faces kept offering to take over, but the offers were declined as everyone involved knew they would be.

As Devin approached, he was stopped by a young woman.

"You know David?" She asked.

Devin wanted to move past her, to not let his mind become distracted, but he remembered the days when he would have to hustle in a similar way.

"What's your name, honey?" He asked her. Her face lit up exposing a new, almost luminous, Hollywood smile.

"Stacey."

"And what do you do?" He hated to ask and saw her face drop as she realised her career so far hadn't made the waves she was promised it would.

"I have a new single out in two weeks. Album's coming in a month." She fought back with a smile. Tough business.

"Put your number in here and I'll do what I can." Devin said. It wasn't a lie, but he knew that he couldn't do much without calling in a lot of favours.

"Thank you so much. Love your blog by the way." He bowed sarcastically and took his phone back. David had spotted the conversation from across the grass, and his eyes locked with Devin's. As if by a telepathic agreement, they met in the middle.

"I can't wait to get off this island." David said.

"Missing your home comforts?"

"Exactly. What can I do for you?"

"Can't I just be catching up with you?" David's eyes said no, and Devin seemed to agree with a nod. "Richard Dickson. Dealt with him much?"

"Only as much as necessary. Why?"

"He's taken a keen interest in you."

"In what way?" As David asked it, his mind was a conveyor belt of all the things Dickson might find if he started digging. He had worried for years about little details of his life slipping out, only to now be in the clutches of someone who might write a whole biography. That's how meticulous Dickson was. He had known he was pushing things too far, but only with cruel hindsight. The truth was he had felt untouchable, and became complacent.

"He thinks you killed Ava." Devin was careful to speak as quietly as possible whilst still being heard. He watched for David's reaction closely, but nothing came – he just stared blankly.

"Are you okay?" Devin asked, reaching a hand out to David's forearm. David took in the people around them quickly and snapped his arm away.

"Get off me." He sneered, quietly but with poison in the words. Devin moved his hand away and took a step back, keeping a fake smile on his face to avoid a scene.

David looked like he was going to apologise, but he didn't. That wasn't unfamiliar for him. He walked away, back towards the campsite. Each step pounded the ground as if he was trying to break it in half.

30

Richard was out of sight, but highly doubted he was out of the minds of everybody on the island. His anxiety began to peak as he realised it was more likely everybody in the UK who had ill wishes for him just now. DI Rankin and DS Donnelly had spent only 2 of the 45 minutes session asking if he was coping with the negative press. The rest was an exercise in making himself trip up over his own story. Fingerprints? Skin samples? Shaky alibis? Prior motive? He had thrown all of those questions at them, even mentioning other names as potential suspects. They didn't come out and say it, but they had nothing but the circumstantial evidence that put Richard in the frame. If there was to be a scape goat, it would be him.

He found a small fence and climbed it, not sure if he was entering or exiting. The grass there, less trodden, made it half-way up his bare shins. Not far ahead was a hedge that ranged from burnt orange, to red, to yellow and finally a deep green. It amazed Richard that something could continue to grow with such little attention. He thought of Ava's influence, and if it would continue. What message would people take from her short life? Or would the roots be snipped by the memory of her murder? Taking a seat by the hedge so that it separated him from any civilization, he took his phone from his pocket. Somewhere along the way it had found some signal – there were voicemails and messages waiting for him. He put it away again, this time taking out his cigarettes and lighting one. The police would be searching for him by now. He knew Rankin would want to keep an eye on him, and his suspicions would be growing stronger with every minute Richard wasn't accounted for. Did De Rossi really want to frame him because he was the killer? Everything pointed that way – the spiked drinks, the set up with Emily, the mysterious meeting at the castle. And yet, there was someone else there that night. Someone Richard was yet to identify. It could be that, as with most of his life, De Rossi was simply a pawn in a larger game. Hayley told him that David had people to do his dirty work – could De Rossi be one of those? Richard shut his eyes and searched for Mary. This time, Ava came. He carried two spirits with him now.

Why did this happen to you? He muttered, closing his eyelids tighter so no light affected the vision of Ava. She was in her red dress, but it wasn't torn or tarnished like it had been on the beach. *Why?* He pleaded again, unsatisfied by her peaceful smile. Her image started to blur and fade, morphing to Mary and back again. Richard's head began to ache and pain flashed in his eyeballs. As Ava disappeared for good, her lips moved but no sound came. Then, like a badly dubbed western, it did. *I was going to help people.* She said. *I was going to show the world the real him.* Her final message was as puzzling and ambiguous as their relationship had been. Helping people was Ava's next move. She wanted to claim the image that she had portrayed over the years. *You fell for it* he pictured her saying, and so he did. In his mind she answered to nothing or nobody, but her journals made it clear that that hadn't been the case. She was under someone's spell. One person, or more? Was *him* a symbol for more than one man in her life? Maybe Richard was included. The secrecy around the island left him feeling dirty. Could the killer be an open secret that only he and the police had been excluded from? And then there was Tara, who was clearly hurt and confused and not being allowed the intimate details of Ava's plans. Tara who, Richard now knew, had fought with Ava on multiple occasions, and who had compromised her son's life to stay by her side for seventeen years. Who kept secrets that even now she wasn't willing to give up. Was she more than an assistant? More than a friend, even?

Whatever their relationship was, Tara had lied to Richard once already – she knew that there was something Ava could do that she wouldn't agree with. That's why she didn't know the next step, because it would involve her. *The year she disappeared* – Tara knew the reasons behind it but seemed adamant in taking them to her grave. David had said that the screaming matches the two of them had were because of Brad, who still stood on the fringes of suspicion. How did Ava's decision to change course stand to affect him? The tears the boy had shed the night before, not far from Richard's shoulder, were ones that had seemed to have built up for years. The fact that Ava's death wouldn't make his life any easier was as clear as glass, but try telling that to a hormonal teenager.

His cigarette was nearing its end, although the wind doing most of the work. It was dry and warm enough for Richard to cause some damage to the hedge behind him with a simple flick. Sometimes all it took was spark. Ava hadn't gotten the chance to start the fire that she was on course to, but Richard was determined to do it for her. Not to clear his own name, but to make sure hers stayed alive. He stubbed the cigarette and put it in his pocket, refusing to leave yet another stain on the beautiful island. Climbing the fence again, and deciding that he was entering this time, he made strides back towards the house. The sun was beginning to float downwards in what felt like the shortest day of his life. As he neared the house, the crowd and the life came into view in the distance, a feeling of finality fell on Richard's shoulders. What was coming to an end though, he didn't know.

A celebrity uprising was a relatively polite affair. It didn't quite hold the menace the same as a protest from the oppressed, or a rally of the wronged. Even still, it was a problem for the detectives and their colleagues. Bobby Taggart stood in front of the crowd as the nominated spokesperson. As always though, he was speaking for himself and only himself. His eyes rarely moved from the luxury yacht that was just off-shore. Between them, though, was DI Rankin.

"Mr Taggart, I appreciate that the investigation has been an inconvenience to you and the other guests here, but a young woman has lost her life." His hands were raised, palms facing outwards. It was a gesture that could either be taken as an apology or a barrier, and it seemed like DI Rankin was aware of the ambiguity.

"So keep the murderer – let the rest of us go."

"That's what I intend to do, but there are questions that remain unanswered and it would make our lives, not to mention the lives of Ava's parents, a whole lot easier if there was cooperation from all parties."

"There's nothing I would love more than upholding the police's stellar reputation, although I have places to be."
Rankin wasn't even attempting to hide his disdain for Bobby Taggart, but what was he to do? He had known from the start that they had a very flimsy grasp of control on the party guests. Now, Taggart's exit would likely be the first of many – the first drop from a soon to be burst pipe. The detective, although frustrated, wasn't about to make the news for a human rights violation. He stepped aside – adding to an extremely short list of times he had done before in his life.

"You'll likely be hearing from us, Mr Taggart." He said as Bobby passed him, flanked by two others. He made sure it was loud enough for most of the crowd to hear.

"I highly doubt that. My lawyers, maybe, but not I."

And with that, Bobby Taggart strode down the slope towards his yacht. A motorized dinghy was on its way to meet him so he didn't get his leather shoes wet. He was dressed for where he was going, not where he had been. The island behind him and the events that had occurred would soon be an anecdote at a cocktail party, a reason to get him invited to a new host of parties. Before he relegated the inconvenience of murder island to his long term memory, he pulled out his phone and sent three messages.

One to Gareth Young: *Don't think you'll be hearing from Rich-*

ard Dickson any time soon. The second went to Paul De Rossi and simply thanked him for the use of his aftershave and a congratulations on the story. The third was to the person who killed Ava Hart. *He's as good as arrested, although I'd worry about the PA. You owe me.* He watched the ticks beside it to make sure it had been read before deleting it.

Back on the island, a phone vibrated in the crowd as DI Rankin and DS Donnelly were attempting to talk the rest of the guests into staying. They had both realised that Donnelly was better served to do the talking.

"Ladies and gentlemen, we understand how upsetting this is, and you're of course free to leave should you have to or choose to." She felt Rankin's eyes on the back of her head, but continued in spite of this. "All we ask is that you cooperate to the best of your knowledge, and unfortunately there are some follow up lines of inquiry that we're now following. Obviously, this will be harder to do if you all go back to your respective sides of the country, or the world for that matter." A few of the LA ladies nodded thanks at being included.

"Do you know who did it?" A voice came from the back of the crowd, boosted in confidence by the anonymity.

"We're getting there. Trust me, we won't rest until we identify and arrest the person who killed Miss Hart." Donnelly glanced around the crowd, meeting eyes with as many individuals as possible. She was making it hard for them to continue their protest. It looked as if she had just bought herself and her colleagues another night, but she wanted to be sure.

"Listen, the sun's almost down and the camp is set up. If you have to organise travel, the safest way to do it is tomorrow. You're not under arrest here, use what's available and we'll get back to work." Donnelly let the warming crowd get to her head a bit, reminding herself that one of the people she was addressing was a cold-blooded killer. Or were they? Richard Dickson was nowhere to be seen, and there was another couple of notable absences.

"If we need to speak to you we'll inform you." She said, trying to end on a note of control. Whether it worked or not was up for debate.

As the group dispersed, mostly reluctantly, she spotted Hayley standing in contemplation. When she arrived, Donnelly thought that that particular megastar may be the most difficult to deal with, but what had transpired was the opposite – often she had seen her looking deflated, and a quick check of her social media feeds showed that she was being one of the most respectful here. Not a hard task, granted, but one that was certainly surprising given her history with the deceased. She kept watching Hayley, aware that she didn't know. It was the best time to try and read someone. She was rotating something in her hand which caught the sun on every turn. An earring? Too small. No, a badge. DS Donnelly approached her.

"Sorry to bother you Miss Dee."

"Call me Hayley." She said, putting the badge into her pocket.

"It's actually that I was going to ask you about." DS Donnelly gestures towards it, seeing Hayley become a touch defensive.

"What about it?"

"It looks like one I found on the beach."

"Makes sense."

"Could I take a look?" Donnelly asked.

Hayley searched briefly for the reason not to hand it over, coming up with nothing. Donnelly took the badge between her fingers and read the message that had been on her mind since the day before. *RE-EMPOWER.* What did it mean? Probably nothing.

"Ava had the same one?" She asked.

"Yeah. Well, both were hers. She gave me this one." Hayley took it back and secured it in her pocket once more.

"Do you know what it means?"

"I wasn't supposed to say."

"Why not?"

"She said I was the only one who she was telling, before -" Hayley looked over towards the horizon, remembering that

Ava's big announcement wouldn't come. The fact that she kept forgetting told her that Ava's death hadn't quite registered yet.

"Hayley, if Ava told you something that night you really need to tell me. It won't make you a suspect." A white lie that would be easily denied if need be.

"It was her next venture. A charity. Support group, she called it." Hayley said.

"Support for what?"

Tears started to form in Hayley's eyes. She didn't bother racing her hands to protect her makeup or turning so nobody could see. She let them flow, because they were for Ava and she deserved as much. Ever since the morning they had found her body, Hayley had felt guilt for ever wishing her ill. She thought back to the party and how fickle she had been, even going as far as plotting her downfall. Of course, all she wanted was her career to suffer a bit, her followers to drop. To make room for Hayley and all that she had planned. She had thought that there wasn't room for both of them, and now she wanted nothing more than to have her rival back.

"It was for abused women. To give them a voice" She told the detective, inhaling deeply to try and stave off a panic attack.

DI Rankin sat across from Brad and Tara, who had demanded to be present. Donnelly would be joining him soon, still calming the mutiny outside. He hadn't gone as far as to admit she was better with dealing with people, but it was clear enough. Besides, he was looking forward to this. Rankin had no time for teenage angst, especially when it was emitted by such a privileged little shit.

"We found some interesting stuff on your mobile, Brad." He said, sliding it into the middle of the table to see if the young man would reach for it. He didn't. A young uniform sat beside him – a local lad. Stubble was starting to grow on the patches that had been clean shaven that morning. He was probably used to herding escaped sheep, a pint with some of the female officers and bed by 10PM. Rankin knew he would be no use, but rules

168

were rules and he wanted everything to be official. Tara shuffled on the seat across from him.

"What do you mean interesting?" She asked.

"I'm not entirely sure you want to present for this."

Tara drew her chair closer into the table to make her decision clear.

"Very well." Rankin checked his notes. "It appears you were Miss Hart's biggest fan, Brad. Too many searches and websites to count."

The reddening of Brad's face began. He knew that he had removed all of his social burner accounts, but had clearly forgotten to clear the history. He stared at the phone and didn't respond.

"And what does that mean? Absolutely nothing. My phone would be the same." Tara said, desperate to hold Brad's hand underneath the table.

"That's true, but you're paid to do that. Or were. Your son on the other hand appears to use his free time to browse pictures of Ava's lingerie shoots. Have you ever heard of fan fiction? I know you have Brad."

The pair of them sat silently, so Rankin continued. A slight smile was forming on the uniform's face.

"Fan fiction is people on the internet writing stories concerning their favourite characters, or celebrities. Now since you refused my invitation to step outside, I'll continue without sparing your blushes. These stories can often play out fantasies. Glorified porn in most cases, and that's what Brad here has been reading. Some real detailed stuff – and not all of it pretty. One particular one had a bit of S&M action, didn't it Brad?" Rankin drilled his eyes into Brad's.

"I didn't read that." Brad spat. "I didn't do anything. People sent me them."

"You didn't enjoy reading them? Maybe light a candle and lock the door?"

"Detective that's wildly inappropriate." Tara said, slapping her palm on the desk.

"Oh believe me I know it is, but it seems to be the truth unfortunately. So Brad, here's what it looks like to me. You had a bit of a fancy for your mum's boss. An unhealthy obsession, we might call it."

"No." He shouted, shaking his head like a dog drying itself.

"Maybe you tried to take your chance at the party – act out one of these stories you were so fond of. Your urges got the better of you. Maybe the S&M story was fresh in your mind."

"Stop it!" Brad took the words out of Tara's mouth. She stood up and lifted him by his hand.

"I suggest you find something more concrete than what a teenage boy does in his spare time, DI Rankin. Until then, I don't want you speaking to my son."

Rankin held his hands up having accomplished exactly what he wanted to. If there was a confession within the boy to be made, it would only take one more talking to. Brad wrestled his hand free, grabbed his phone and swung the door open so it battered against the wall. Tara followed with quick steps, but it was clear he was on his way out the door and into the island. His phone pinged as he went, sending his embarrassment into overdrive.

When they were alone, the young cop switched off the recording equipment and looked at Rankin.

"So these stories…"

"Make yourself scarce, son." Ranking told him.

He nodded and scurried away, leaving his hat behind. Rankin leant back and felt like he was finally getting somewhere. The boy knew something. He had went from 200 suspects and was down to two. Now where was Richard Dickson?

31

Tara had second-hand embarrassment, but more so she felt sick. Had he really been obsessed with Ava? It felt wrong on countless levels, and yet she couldn't blame him. He knew no better, and didn't have a father figure to teach him the respect she wished he had. For the first time in her life, the feeling of being in control was like sand in between fingertips. She followed him as his pace picked up and he made his way through the curious crowd. They were all thinking that the police had found the killer. She couldn't help but wonder too…

An incoming call distracted her long enough to lose sight of him. When she saw the name on the screen she had no choice but to answer.

"Mrs Hart. I'm so sorry." She said, thankful that she wasn't face to face with the caller.

"Oh Tara. How could this happen?" Ava's mum hadn't called since the news, but Tara knew that it would come at one point.

"I wish I had more to tell you. I wish you weren't going through this."

Ava's mum responded by simply breaking down. Tara held the phone away from her ear to eliminate the force of the sobbing. After a minute or so, she caught her breath and spoke again.

"The police were here last night." She told Tara.

"I know. It's hard to understand how they aren't any further forward."

"The man was an oaf. But listen, darling – you were always so kind to us and great for Ava. You kept her grounded. Made her check in with us."

Tara had a lump in her throat that halted any response.

"I just wanted to phone you and ask whether or not we should have told them about - you know…"

"Please, leave it up to me." Tara interrupted.

"Okay, we didn't say anything."

"Thank you. Listen, can I phone back? It's just they're calling me back in for questioning." Tara lied.

"You poor girl."

The tears were starting again. Tara managed to say goodbye quietly and end the call. Ava's biggest secret was safe for now, but it wouldn't be long until her mother caved, Tara knew it. All she could do before she did was start to deal with it herself. That meant betraying Ava's trust, and throwing her own life into havoc for good measure. *Oh Ava* she thought – *it was good while it lasted.* Now, on top of everything else, Brad was nowhere to be seen.

"And why the fuck has she only told us this now?" DI Rankin was pacing in the hallway as he was updated. Hayley was seated in the dining room with a mug of herbal tea.

"I'm not sure – maybe she didn't know what would happen with it now? Respect her memory, that sort of thing. I think she was thinking about what to do." DS Donnelly heard herself sticking up for Hayley, who she knew Rankin would now be putting back in the frame as a suspect. That was the right thing to do, but she had a strong sense that Hayley was innocent in all of this.

"So what does it tell us?" *He always does this*, she thought – *makes it look as if he's thinking out loud but really just getting me to tell him what I know.*

"Well, a charity for abused women – not exactly new is it? But if she had some sort of focus on the showbiz industry, which seems likely, I'm sure it would put the fear into a lot of men. A kind of day of reckoning."

"Didn't that already happen?"

"Barely scratched the surface, sir."

DI Rankin nodded, still as out of his depth as when he started reading into Ava's modern day celebrity lifestyle.

"Richard Dickson had a brief foray into something similar recently." DI Rankin mused. "And it didn't go down well."

"Some say his false accusations hurt the fight more than helped it." DS Donnelly concurred.

"Maybe Ava brought him here to make an example of him? He found out, confronted her and it got out of hand?"

They stood in silence, neither prepared to throw their weight behind that particular theory just yet. DI Rankin looked out the window and was met by almost complete darkness. The nights here seemed to take over as if a switch had been flicked. Roars from the engines of a few quad bikes came into ear shot and he sighed.

"Don't worry, sir – a couple of the local boys are keeping an eye on things."

"There's a murderer out there." Rankin said, almost embarrassed at the way his investigation was going.

"A moment that got out of hand, no?" DS Donnelly asked.

"Let's hope so."

"Want me to find Dickson?" Donnelly asked.

"Let's get all the details from this one first. He can't get far."

"Okay. How did it go with Brad?"

"He was suitably embarrassed. Ran off into the night. Still, if we considered every young boy who'd had a wank over Ava Hart we'd have queues the length of Scotland. We need more."

Donnelly baulked at the sentence, and he held a hand up to apologise.

"Maybe you should lead on this one." Rankin said, as they entered the room to speak to Hayley.

Finally realising how vast the island actually was, Richard was lost. He had spent an hour on the phone to his dad, speaking through gritted teeth and trying with all his might to keep his temper at bay. It had quickly turned from concern into a lecture. His mum would say *it's just his way of showing you her cares*, but his mum wasn't here. He managed to end the call with a goodbye rather than hanging up in silence. Now, alone and with no lights in sight, he had no idea if he was going the right way. What was the right way anyway? Back to the mob who thought he was a murderer? A confrontation with De Rossi? Now, at his lowest point, all that was keeping the suicidal thoughts away was the fact that he wouldn't be able to defend himself against the suspicion. Quad bikes in the distance. A group of them, so nothing to be worried about. He walked towards the rumble. His back felt exposed to the darkness, so he started to jog. Despite the lack of fitness, sleep and strength, it was a steady pace. Before he knew it, the air changed around him. A panicked presence. Where was it coming from? All angles around him looked the same. Looking back and moving forwards, he collided with whoever it was.

"Brad?" Tara squealed, picking herself up from the ground. Richard did the same, his knee aching from the fall.

"Tara, it's me – Richard." With that, the darkness seemed to subside slightly. Their senses were gathered.

"Fuck. I have no idea where he is."

"It's okay, don't panic yet. He was out and about last night. I met him at the castle."

"The castle? On his own? Why?" Tara's breathing was frantic, as if she hadn't let her son out of her sight like this for seventeen years.

"I don't know – to clear his head? My point is, he was fine."

"You have to help me find him, he shouldn't be out there on his own with..."

"I know." Richard said. She couldn't bring herself to mention the killer. Richard thought that nobody had really considered a second attack, but the slightest oddity could change that.

"Which way's the house?"

"Wherever I came from."

"Okay so we'll go that way together. When we know where we are, I'll check the castle." Richard said.

"He asked me how to get to the lighthouse earlier." Tara added.

"Well that's where we'll go."

Tara nodded, accepting his arm, and they walked.

"I'm sure he's fine." Richard said, finding nothing else suitable. She didn't respond but held tighter as they tried their best to avoid divots and bumps.

"Does he disappear like this often?"

"No, he's very attached to us. To me." She corrected herself.

"So Ava cared for him, too?"

"She did what she could to help. They had a strange relationship – I think Brad had a bit of a crush on her. You know, in that childish sort of way – he would love her one minute and hate her the next." She hated lying, but she had to justify the crush as childish for fear of more bouts of vomiting.

"How did she feel about that?"

"Awkward, I suppose. She just wanted to make sure he was okay."

"He was talking about his Dad last night."

Tara seemed resigned to the fact that that particular conversation would never go away. In fact, it would likely become more frequent as Brad grew older. She went to speak a couple of times but failed.

"Did something happen to you, Tara?" Richard could sense tears but it was too dark to be sure. Her grip on his arm had loosened a bit, but she was still holding on. Could this be why Ava was so interested in Jane? Had her best friend been abused?

"It's not what you think." Tara said, lifting her free arm to her face confirming the tears. Engine roars came from the distance. In the dark, they sounded menacing. "People have gone a bit rogue – the police were struggling to keep everyone on the island earlier."

"Brad said that he thought he might be here, on the island?" Richard was too exhausted to let her change the subject. He posed it as a question, but wouldn't bet on getting an answer.

They were getting closer to the noise now, and it sounded like something from a post-apocalyptic film. Whoops and hollers, roaring and skidding. From their vantage point, they could see a group of headlights driving around a small clearing. It unsettled

Richard how little space they took up. Since he'd been there the island had seemed small, almost claustrophobic. Before, he had wondered how it was possible that nobody heard Ava struggle or scream, now it was obvious that the sounds had been quite easily lost to the night. Surrounded by the people she thought were closest to her, and unable to let any of them know the danger she was in. Or were they the closest people to her? De Rossi, Hayley, Bobby Taggart, potentially Brad's father – it wasn't a celebration at all. Tara's phone rang, startling them both. She tried to tell Richard that it was Brad before answering, but it just came out as a mumble.

"Hello? Brad?" On the other side, Richard heard the one thing he was hoping not to – panic. He could almost make out three words. *Lost. Sorry. Scared.* He spun around looking and listening for any signs of him. Apart from their view down to the quadbikes, which were still circling each other, it was futile – too many dunes, dips and cliffs. The wind was picking up too, meaning any noise from certain directions was being swept off the cliffs and into the ocean. Tara was barking at Brad to calm down and describe his location. Again, there was no chance of that, but she was laser focused on continuing. It was hard for her organised and practical mind to accept that words and plans wouldn't cut it here. They needed to search quickly and blindly. Richard tried to encourage the feeling that this was a moment of panic that would soon be over – Brad probably wasn't far – but it was overshadowed by something more sinister. Life had beaten him into finally expecting the worst because that's what it had turned out to be every time before.

"Don't move, and don't get back on the bike. I'm coming." Tara said into the phone, failing in her attempts to remain calm and not worry Brad more. His meek response sounded like a child crying for his mother – all the brooding teenage years had disappeared and he was a baby again. Richard had seen flashes of it the night before.

"Is he on his own?" Richard asked, glancing towards the group of anonymous headlights again. Tara nodded. Her eyes shot around between seconds of focus, the bright blue pupils moving like fish in an unfamiliar tank. It would be pointless to ask if he had described where he was in any revealing detail.

"This is going to be okay – we'll find him."

"There are things you don't know about Brad. Things that nobody knows. You asked if it had anything to do with the murder and honestly, I didn't think it could. But now - " She looked at Richard, ready to reveal it all. A singular engine roar came from somewhere towards their left, miles from the other bikes. Tara ran towards it.

32

Richard used his phone as a spotlight. The black vignette circling everything he could see added menace to the night. He had lost Tara now, having been certain that she was running alongside him. He wanted to catch up with her for more than one reason – his fear being high up on the list. Trying to regulate his breathing, he searched for another source of light, however far away it may be. Nothing. The hills were engulfing him in darkness. Why had Tara been so worried about Brad? It wasn't just a mother's instinct – there was a reason she thought that the killer might target him next. Why, Richard had no idea. As far as he was concerned he had barely anything to do with her. Had Ava known his father? Had she planned to reunite them this weekend? Too many things were buzzing in his mind and not enough was around him to steal his concentration. This was just like when Mary was snatched from him as a child – something bad was happening in front of his eyes and he didn't know what or why. His hands stung, his knee hurt and his eye pulsed along with the beat of his heart. He remembered this feeling – it was defeat. Scared to move in case it was in the wrong direction, Richard slumped onto a mound of grass beside him. Sleep had never felt further away, and yet it was the only thing that would keep him sane. He raised his fists as the roar of a quad bike came in and then out of earshot. Somebody knew where they were going.

Tara kept one eye on the uneven terrain as she brought up Brad's number on the screen. No signal. She kept moving. Her life had fallen apart in the space of 24 hours, and the destruction showed no signs of stopping. Brad was all she had left, and she swore to herself that she would protect him in Ava's memory. That was about as far as her grieving had got, but she knew that when she had a moment of peace without worry or sickness that she would cry for days. No time now, though – Brad needed her. Her instincts were taking her towards the edge of the island with no reasoning as to why. Out of the long grass and hills, the wind picked up so much that it hurt her ear drums.

Tara's glasses slipped down her nose. She cursed herself for still not getting them tightened – one of a number of personal errands that had been knocked off her list by Ava's. Her eyes felt dry and sore as they always did. Then she found herself cursing Ava in general. She wouldn't have been able to travel the world without her, but she also wouldn't have ended up here, like this. Brad wouldn't be lost and afraid. As she jogged towards the cliffs, she thought back to the argument they had about him coming. "He can stay with my parents." Tara had said. But no – Ava insisted he came to the island. This fucking cursed island. She was finally realising that he was a part of her plan – the one she had refused to let Tara in on. Why? Because she would've talked her out of it. How could she use Brad after everything Tara had done for her? Everything she had done for both of them? His picture flashed up on her phone screen. Cursed indeed, she thought. The picture was a few years old – his face still smooth and without the rash from a razor. Ava had told him if he shaved everyday his beard would come in faster. His hair was shorter too, not like the feminine cut he had now. Another one of Ava's ideas. There was a rare smile on his face.

"Brad? Where are you? I'm on my way."
"Mum." His voice sounded raw. The signal came and went.
"He ... meet me."
"Who wants to meet you? Brad, stay exactly where you are. Don't go and meet a soul." She wanted to sound stern and in control. The result was much different.

"I'm … edge of the … too dark."

"Brad, stay where you are."

"Who … and … Dad."

"Brad you're emotional – I'll tell you everything, I promise. Just tell me where you are."

The line cut out. It took all of Tara's strength to not throw her phone towards the ocean. She halted suddenly, feet skidding and stopping her from running off the edge. Jagged rocks that looked like they could slice through skin pointed up at her. The wind, following no rules, blew her back towards the land and then tried to take her over the edge. Where was the house? Where was Richard? Where was Brad? She tried his number again, but heard the most painful three beeps of her life. Each one felt like a punch to the kidney. *I promised to keep him safe. Don't give up now.* She whispered, mustering every bit of composure she had gained over the last eighteen years. Someone was playing games with him, and she couldn't bear to think of what the goal might be. He was out in the open, that was for sure. The wind and waves on the call were almost as audible as his voice. She shone the phone's torch to the ground and skirted the edge, giving herself a couple of metres of space from it. *God, Ava, what have you done?* What could she possibly have needed to do with her life at this point that would put them all in this much danger? For the best part of twenty years, they hadn't gone more than a couple of days without being together.

At one point, Tara had considered that they might be more than friends. Years later they laughed about that. She had watched from the sidelines as Ava took over the world and gained everything a young girl could ever dream of. And yet, she held onto hate in her heart. The episodes of tears and shrieks during the night, whilst rare, proved it. Tara could count on one hand the number of secrets Ava had kept from her, and her past trauma was one. The identity of *him* was another, but maybe they were the same thing. As she picked up the pace, she promised that if she could leave this island unscathed, she would tell someone the secret that had shaped her adult years. The secret

Brad so desperately wanted to know. The secret, she was beginning to suspect, which led to Ava's murder.

"Tara." The end of her name carried on into the night like somebody's final scream. It was the wind playing tricks on her.

"Hello?" She shouted back. "Hello?" Louder now.

"Tara?" It was further away this time. She couldn't be sure, but it sounded like Richard.

"Over here." She shouted again, her throat aching.

"Tara?" Quieter still, almost impossible to hear at all. Tara tried to whistle but it quickly turned into a breathless cough.

If he was still shouting her name, he was too far away for her to know. She had to carry on. Brad was all she had now, and all that was left to remind her of Ava. A light in the distance caught her eye. Richard's torch? She stopped on the spot and tried to focus her eyes on it. It grew larger on its way towards her. Not a torch, but a headlight. The growl of the bike came not long after. One, two, three revs of the engine. The light grew bigger and brighter still.

"Brad?" She shouted, almost losing her voice completely now. Or it could be the police. Either way, she would take the help. That was assuming that whoever it was wanted to help... The bike curved down a hill and towards her. All she could make out was a hunched silhouette. "I need help" She said, defeatedly, as if she was talking to nobody. Then, she screamed like never before in her life. The noise was deafening as the quad bike skimmed past her. She felt the presence and smelled the body. It wasn't Brad. But who? As soon as Tara noticed it turning to come back for her once more, she ran. Her light flashed back and forwards as her arms propelled her and she drew on breath she didn't know she had. The noise was growing again – she had no chance. She threw a glance over her shoulder one last time to try and identify her stalker. Darkness still. The bike was metres away from her now as she reached a full sprint. In seconds, her heels would be caught under the thick rubber wheels. Instead, she chose flight. Tara dived to her side and over the edge. Before she collided with the rocks down below, she heard the quad bike continue on. Within seconds, Tara's glasses were swallowed by the waves.

33

Chief Inspector Murphy wanted off the island. He had taken the night shift, despite it being well below his pay grade, to give some of his officers a break. The people here, their lifestyle, their pleasures – he didn't understand it. If he was on the mainland and out in a patrol car, which he still often did to pass the time, he'd be talking the local kids out of some vandalism or taking the keys off an old pal who was about to get behind the wheel after six pints. Instead he was watching his footing in case of sheep shit or a bump on the ground, in that order of importance. A poor girl was dead, and they were keeping her peers hostage so the Glasgow city boys could solve a murder in record time. That wasn't the policing he knew, nor one was he comfortable with. *Get the journalist. Not the fat one.* DI Rankin said to him. Where you were from clearly held more importance than rank in his world. Murphy did well not to put him in his place. Unnecessary stress, his wife Cheryl would call it. Better to stay quiet and help when you can. He longed to be lying beside her in bed just now, both reading their books. History was his thing, crime fiction hers. He often scoffed at the storylines she would recap for him. Things don't happen like that, he told her. Wait until she hears all about this. His instincts were transported back to the island when he heard Richard.

"Tara." He shouted.

"Not Tara, son. Come here." Murphy could see him now. A stumbling mess. He again remembered him crashing onto the beach on the morning that they found Ava's body. The short amount of time since hadn't been kind to him – he looked as if he was rotting from the inside.

"Let's get you back to some warmth." It was a cold night indeed. This part of the country had a tendency to trick you into thinking it wouldn't be.

"She's still out there. She's looking for her son." Richard said, seemingly protesting but sliding his arm under Murphy's.

"You can barely walk – are you hurt?"

"My knee's feeling a bit achy. We need to find Tara. She thinks she's in danger." At that, Murphy stopped.

"In danger how, son?"

"I know about as much as you, but she sounded pretty convinced." Richard said, breathlessly.

Murphy sized him up. As dismissive as he was about the Glasgow way of doing things, he was just as close as them to piecing together this puzzle. He could understand why others on the island suspected Richard – he turned up wherever there was trouble. Murphy? He still felt that the journalist was the only one here outside of a uniform that cared about finding the killer. He didn't buy the tabloid gossip. If anything, it made it less likely. Still, he grasped Richard's arm a bit tighter, just enough to be in control should he need to be. He'd be a bloody laughing stock if his hunch was wrong. With his free hand, he held down the button on his radio.

"This is Murphy. We're missing a young woman by the name of Tara. Can we get a couple out to search for her?" He clicked off.

"And her son, Brad."

"And her young boy – Brad." Murphy said into the radio.

A confirmation came back on the radio, and he turned his attention back to Richard. The man looked like he'd fallen between two boats and battered off the sides on the way down.

"Let's get you a coffee." Murphy said, projecting his desires. Richard just nodded.

"What are you doing out here anyway?"

"I had to get some space to think." Richard answered.

"Did you get enough? We're miles out from the campsite."

"If I did, it didn't work."

"Trying to play detective?"

Richard bit his tongue, wanting to say that somebody had to. Murphy sensed it.

"I know it's frustrating, you lost your friend. We'll get the bastard." The officer told him.

"There's something going on. Something with Brad. I'm sure of it."

"Let's get you a seat and you can tell me what you know."

Richard's phone vibrated. Murphy let him stop and allowed him use of his arm. After all, it could be Tara - but it wasn't. He tapped open the email he had requested the day before and pictures of Ava as a young woman slowly faded onto the screen. Murphy looked over his shoulder and let him mourn for a minute. He scrolled through the pictures. There he was on the screen too, even goofier back then without the weight he had put on in the time since. Pictures of Ava performing on stage. Pictures of the two of them together. Group shots. A few familiar faces from the island, much fresher of course. He stopped at one, and zoomed in as far as the phone would allow him. Could that be *him*? The source of Ava's angst?

"Come on now, son." Murphy took his arm again, but his eyes didn't leave the screen. *Son.* Richard thought. They trudged on. Ava's young face and naïve smile looked back at him from the phone screen. Strangely, his strength had returned. There was something about the picture that wanted to tell him more. He couldn't quite unlock it yet.

Rankin looked himself in the mirror as the voice on the other end of the line grew louder. His Chief Inspector had heard about Bobby Taggart leaving the island, and had already been on the receiving end of a call from his lawyers. He wouldn't get a bollocking like that without passing it on, so it ended up in Rankin's ear.

"Sir -" He tried to cut in, but was shot down immediately, nodding an apology even though he was locked away in the bathroom on his own. He was the last person who had to be told that the pressure was mounting. It was all over the press, there was a mutiny brewing and he was no closer to catching a killer. No closer? Could that really be true? It was pitiful really. The old saying *it's like shooting fish in a barrel* came to his mind, yet here he was with his harpoon pointed squarely at it and he couldn't catch a thing. Ava's parents had been distraught, taking their anger out on him and DS Donnelly. She did well to console them and bring them back to the conversation at hand, but they had nothing to offer. If they did, they were keeping it to themselves. No feuds, no lovers, no past enemies out for revenge. It didn't help that they knew little of what their daughter even did. They saw her on the TV more than in person, and Rankin imagined that they'd have it on mute as they reminisced about her younger years and how much she'd grown up. There was a knock at the door. It took him a few seconds to realise that the Chief had hung up a minute before – the phone was still pressed to his ear. He pocketed it.

"Yes?"

"Sir, Dickson is here." DS Donnelly said, loud enough so others could hear. Probably to put the fear into Richard. She'd make a good detective yet, he thought, before composing himself and unlocking the door. Richard Dickson looked as if a 4x4 had hit him and took him through the car wash.

"In here." Rankin said, simply. He felt a bit sorry for the journalist – there was a bollocking due to passed down and he was the man it would fall on next. He sat down at the table that DI Rankin was beginning to despise. It had given him splinters and wobbled as he took notes. The darkness outside was all encompassing now, sneaking up on the island for the third night in a row.

"Care to explain why we couldn't find you?" He chose to stand, Donnelly taking the seat across from Richard.

"Listen, I think Brad is in danger."

"The boy? Why?"

"I was out there, walking, and I bumped into Tara. She couldn't find him, but he had phoned her in a state. He was lost."

"And you just happened to be in the vicinity?"

186

"I just happened to be in the vicinity." Richard said, with a bit of acid in his tone.

"Seems to happen to you a lot. Now there comes a point where I begin to think that it's not trouble following you – it's that you bring it with you."

"We don't have time for this – he could be hurt out there. He could be..." Richard couldn't bring himself to say it.

"He could be what?" Rankin pushed, leaning on the table with enough force to stop the wobble.

"There's a murderer out there – do I have to spell it out?"

"As I understand it, we've officers looking for the two of them." He looked to Donnelly for confirmation, who nodded once. "So, any proof that you were with his Mother looking for him?"

"No, no proof." A long sigh escaped from Richard. His mind seemed to be focused elsewhere.

"Journalists like you should know better – always need to back your stories up."

As Richard contemplated how to reply, seemingly between complete rage and slight anger, a young uniform knocked and popped her head round the door. Rankin sent Donnelly with a flick of his head. He wasn't letting Richard out of his sight. He knew that with a few more digs a confession might come.

"You asked her for help, didn't you?" Richard didn't respond, but held Rankin's stare.

"You asked Ava Hart for help and she told you where to go." The detective continued. "That was your last shot – your old pal who has a bit of clout now. She was your only way back into the good grace's of the public. Except you don't belong there, Dickson. You're as bad as the rest of them. And you proved it by lashing out when she turned you down. That's what happened, isn't it? Maybe it got out of hand – maybe you didn't mean for her to die – but she did. It's only a matter of time 'til I nail you, son. Make my life easier for me. Tell me that's what happened." He had lost the plot, his anger getting the better of him. What was worse was that Richard saw it happening.

He simply stared back at the detective, silently willing him to go further. Before the tension could erupt, Donnelly came back into the room.

"Sir, a word?" Rankin seemed to consider staying, but relented and left the room. Behind the door, he drew a long breath, not caring if Donnelly saw his frustration. She gave him a moment before speaking, and he took it.

"Tell me we've got something." He said, keeping his eyes shut and leaning against the wall.

"Maybe, sir. That was Ava Hart's mother on the phone. Seems you were right – they were holding something back."

Rankin straightened himself slowly like a drunk off a railing. Could this be the break he needed?

"Ava Hart was pregnant, sir."

"Jesus Christ, how far along?" How the fuck had they not spotted that in the lab? This would be a scandal like they'd never seen before.

"Not now, sir. Before. When she was eighteen. Her mother said she never told them who the father was, only that she put the baby up for adoption."

"Eighteen?"

"Sir." Donnelly nodded.

"Just as well we have her high school sweetheart sweating in the other room then, isn't it DS Donnelly. And now, he has a motive."

34

Richard was quietly having an epiphany. When he first entered a newsroom at 20 years old, it took only minutes for him to realise that the industry he had been idolizing for years was no different than any other he had experienced. There were coffee stains on the tables, people were copied into emails by accident and, largely, most of the staff were blagging their way through work whilst letting all of their personal dramas seep in throughout the shift. It was, as with everything else in life, messy. Through his work he had quickly found out that politics and government were the same. Sure, the people began to sound more sure of themselves and their actions, but they were as clueless as the rest of us. Up until now he had held science and policing to a higher regard – the last two hopes of people in charge actually knowing what to do and how to do it. He had lost a lot on this island so far, but would leave having gained the knowledge that law and order, like the media and like the government, were as human as the rest of us. There was always science, he thought, leaning back on the chair and hoping with all his might that Tara had found Brad and they were in the safe, if flawed, arms of the police. He should be out there searching instead of sitting here being framed for the murder of his childhood sweetheart.

DI Rankin and DS Donnelly came back in. He couldn't be sure, but he thought he caught a hop in the step of the weathered detective. DS Donnelly looked determined but unsure – the inner workings of her mind playing out through long blinks and quick glances around the room. She took the seat she had vacated not five minutes before, and clicked the recording equipment back on, giving a brief note of recommencement for the benefit of a future audience.

"Mr Dickson." DI Rankin said, deciding to stay standing again. "Have you ever had sexual relations with Ava Hart?" Richard began to blush like a puberty struck child during sex education.

"Haven't we been through this? We were together towards the end of high school. I can hardly see what it has to do with just now."

"At the age of eighteen?"

"Yes, at the age of eighteen."

"And you engaged in sexual relations?"

"I mean, as much as a teenage boy can engage in sexual relations, yes."

Rankin nodded, getting the confirmation he so desired. He noted something down on a sheet of paper in front of him. For all Richard knew it could've been a doodle. He took the silence as an opportunity to direct the detective's attention to Tara and Brad.

"Listen, there's something going on out there. You think you've got a killer sitting in front of you, but I can assure you that he's out there." He gestured to the window, noticing that the darkness had completely taken over now. Some phone screens illuminated the campsite, matching with a few stars in the sky. The rest was black and blue.

"I'll tell you again Mr Dickson that our officers are dealing with it." DI Rankin drilled his eyes into Richard's. "Were you aware that Miss Hart fell pregnant around the time that your relationship ended?" Both detectives were laser focused on his reaction, which came slowly. It began with a scoff, before deep thought and confusion took over.

"You're wrong." Richard said. It was painfully quiet.

"Oh I can assure you that we're not. Admission from Miss Hart's parents tells us that we're dead right. Soon we'll have all the details we need to pin you down as the absent father. Granted, it got past us initially, but now we know you'll understand that we have a few more questions for you."

Ava pregnant? He challenged his mind to take him back to the night that they slept together, but it offered nothing new. It was over quickly, uncomfortable and they had laughed about it later. Would she really not tell him? Could it be the reason for the distance over the years?

"Did she have an abortion?" He felt sick saying it – talking about a dead friend in such a callous way.

"I think you know that she didn't." Rankin said, finding no sentiment in the fact that he may have just informed a man that he was a father. "I think that the child being adopted and taken from you has eaten at you over the years. That's what I think. You came here to settle a score, maybe get the information you've been chasing for the past 17 years. But she wouldn't give it to you it." Richard was shaking his head as Rankin continued, his voice rising steadily. "You pleaded with her but it got out of hand. You were angry. Drunk. Lost."

"No." Richard said.

"You lashed out and that's all she wrote." Rankin slammed his hand down on the table, startling nobody but making his point nonetheless.

Richard tried to put the puzzle together in his head but he was left with pieces from different boxes. Could this be the key to everything that had happened here? Could he really be the father of someone out there in the world just now? What would they be like? Ava, hopefully. He had a hundred questions in a room with people who wanted answers instead.

"Here's what's going to happen -" Rankin was interrupted by a panic outside. DS Donnelly's radio pleaded for assistance. All Richard could make out was *unconscious and bleeding*. Tara? Brad? Rankin looked like he was genuinely considering ignoring it to try and get a confession out of Richard. His better judgement won in the end.

"Don't move." He warned him, as the two detectives left the room to potentially be met with their dreaded second victim.

The door sat ajar behind them, and Richard moved towards it to gather what he could from the commotion. As his eyes found the space, he saw a body being brought into the house on a stretcher. The left leg was twisted beyond normal function. A dainty leg, so Tara rather than her son. No sign of him. Maneuvering her around, her face came close to the door. A single sharp breath told Richard she was fighting to stay alive, but his mind was elsewhere. Tara had lost her glasses. Her left eye was as he remembered it, piercing blue like Brad's and Ava's. Like his own as well. Her right, the one that had evidently lost the contact lens, was a deep brown.

Richard's phone vibrated on the table causing him to leap backwards, hoping not to draw any attention to himself or his room. Anonymous. He answered.

"Hello?"

A clearing of the throat. A silent consideration of the words that were to come.

"Who is this?"

"I'm sorry you've not heard from me." It was Jane – another frayed thread of his life that needed some attention. Richard had come to the island to forget all about it, and it had worked, but not in the way that he wanted – new trauma now replaced it. He was almost certain that he didn't have the capacity to speak to Jane just now. There were answers he needed from her, and yet he didn't blame her for anything at all. She had gotten further than most in telling her story of assault and manipulation. In this case, falling at the last hurdle said more about the race than it did about the horse.

"Jane?" He asked, buying himself some time. She deserved every bit of his attention and care at the very least. It was something he couldn't give her. Not now. And yet, he needed her should he ever want to clear his name, assuming he ever got off the island.

"I'm sorry you've not been able to get me. I've just been - I don't really have an excuse." Richard was transported back to his life before Ava's murder, and reminded starkly that it wasn't going all that well even then. Jane, it seemed, still had faith in him. She obviously didn't read the tabloids.

"It's okay. I didn't think I'd ever hear from you again. Did I – was it something I did? I've been going over it in my head constantly." He decided he had to take the opportunity, considering she could go off grid for months again.

"No. It all got a bit much – I'm a bit lost with it, but I didn't say what they said I did. I didn't mean for you to suffer, honestly."

It was clear Jane couldn't win. Maybe she was paid off – something Richard wouldn't blame her for accepting. Everyone likes to think they'd become a martyr, but when the opportunity actually presents itself the decision is much more difficult.

"Are you still there?" She asked, her voice as fragile as everything else in her life.

"Yeah. Listen, can we meet soon? Maybe it would be better to work everything out in person. The story doesn't matter." He avoided thinking about whether or not he would leave the island a free man.

"Okay. I'd still like you to – you know… one day you can tell my story?" She posed it as a question, as if to seek approval that it was one worth telling.

It was a sign to Richard that her confidence had been beaten down and boxed in to the point that she felt that somehow she didn't matter as much as anybody else. It wasn't Jane he was thinking about though. He was thinking about the last person who had asked him that question in that way.

35

Breaking out was easy. Everyone's attention seemed to be on reviving Tara to find out what happened to her. Richard couldn't hang around long enough to find out what her chances were. What he did know was that no matter the cuts and breaks, her secret would be kept for a while longer. Maybe what had happened now would finally get her to open up about what her and Ava had kept from the world. After all, and despite her thinking otherwise, it was what caused Ava's death. Luckily, with the help of an old picture, a missing contact lens and the revelation of a fatherless child, Richard had stumbled on the answer. He looked at the picture he had been sent one more time as he made his way round the back of the house. Ava's smile was innocently beautiful. With her braces recently removed, she had just been getting used to showing teeth again. Richard stood off to the side, gangly and awkward. His eyes looked out to the side towards her, quietly calculating what her talent meant for their young love. That was the day she had been *discovered*. Looking at it he saw the past play out, including everything that Ava had taken to her early grave. She was ready to change that, and it would've been devastating for many. For days Richard had tried to get into her mind and look at where her path was heading. The announcement she had planned to make had never revealed itself, until now.

The quad bike was there to take him into the unknown, the keys in the ignition willing him to go. He had to get to Brad. Richard's body jerked backwards as the bike took off. The engine noise joined in with the other bikes driving around the house.

They would help him stay incognito as he passed through the pack and out on his own. There was one stop he had to make. David's tent was the most extravagant of the lot. Some would call it glamping rather than camping. The entrance was zipped shut but he heard some hushed tones as he approached. He left the bike a bit further away so as not to announce his presence more than he had to. Unzipping it quickly, he was faced with something that hadn't crossed his mind at all – David on top of Devin, shirtless and red-faced.

"What the fuck?!" He reacted before turning around to see who was watching, but the fact that anyone was there at all was enough.

"Jesus – sorry. You can't really knock on a tent but I did give it a try."

"Get the fuck out."

"So you never did have a relationship with Ava?" Richard said.

"Of course I didn't."

"But it was convenient not to come out and say it? Pardon the pun."

"What is it you want?" David was standing now and taking Richard outside as Devin got dressed. There was no activity around, which was presumably a factor in choosing the location.

"Ava was Brad's real mother?"

"Did the little fucker kill her?" David asked.

"Ava was Brad's mother?" Richard repeated, already wasting time he didn't have. Of course, he knew he was right. The picture he had from the talent showed similarities between the two that were hard to argue against.

"Yes, Dickson. She was."

"And what do you know about the father?"

David looked at Richard, this time without spluttering back an irritated answer. He smiled slightly.

"It's you isn't it?" He asked Richard.

Richard sighed and turned away, his head in his hands. How could the people closest to her not know? Between them, Tara and David knew more about Ava than anybody else in the world

– yet they didn't know who fathered the child that her assistant raised for her, presumably to keep her career on track.

"No it's not me."

"She said it was an old boyfriend. A nobody. I just figured – you know." David shrugged and looked him up and down.

"And Tara – she wanted to take care of him? She was only young herself."

"There were arguments sometimes, but it seemed like an okay situation. In a fucked-up sort of way. They were a partnership like you've never seen before."

"Ava was fine with not being there for him? Raising him?"

"As far as I could tell she didn't want him in the beginning. When she started growing up, you could say that there was something like love there." David glanced back to Devin who was still lying on the ground.

"So her hiatus wasn't a mental breakdown – it was a pregnancy and some recovery?" Richard got his attention back.

"Bit of both I'd say. But yes – she needed time to lose the weight."

The line made Richard want to swing for David, but he know he was just embodying the industry itself. Equality was talked about, but it was nowhere near implemented. A fact proven by Ava, the strongest woman he knew, bowing to the pressures around her. It took her almost 20 years to muster the strength, the power, to take control. Almost.

"You never thought that all of this could be because of the real father?"

"He's not made an appearance for 18 years – why start now? It's not like Brad's the most charming young man."

But David was wrong. Richard knew that he had made plenty of appearances over the years. He turned to go, getting nothing from David other than the opinions of a clown.

"Wait, Richard." David called him back. He obliged, turning and hoping for one last piece of advice before he went to confront a murderer.

"Is this, you know – me and him – going to end up in the

papers?"

"Get over yourself, you idiot." Was all Richard could muster. "You know the killer would be in jail by now if you all here weren't so damn worried about your selves."

He got back on the bike – revving and pushing the machine to its limit – whatever happened he knew he would never ride one of these again, and wouldn't be surprised if the mere sound of an engine gave him PTSD. Brad had been looking for the lighthouse, and Richard hoped he would be on his way there now. He didn't even want to consider him already being there. Even if Tara hadn't been attacked, which he assumed she had been, she would never have found him because she had been on the wrong side of the island. The lighthouse seemed fitting. A relic of the past clinging on to the future – much like the person he expected to see when he arrived. As the bike's wheels left the ground for a split second coming off a mound of grass, Richard spotted Brad. He braked and turned, almost flipping the machine on its side. Brad, taken out of his trance, jumped backwards and squinted to identify him.

"It's me – Richard."

"You?" There was hope in his tone. Just as Richard had suspected, he was headed to the lighthouse to meet his father.

"No, not me. I mean, I'm not the one playing games with you. You know that's all it is, don't you?"

"He told me my dad was at the lighthouse." Brad's eyelids looked like tears had been taking their toll most of the day, and were about to return once more. The teenage angst was a good front for an emotionally wrecked and damaged kid.

"Brad, I know you don't know me well, but I know a bit about you. Someone's using you – trust me. You've got your mum here, and she's hurt. She needs you right now."

"Mum's hurt?"

"She is, and you could be too if you keep going."

Brad thought about it for a minute. He had been so caught up in his own quest that he seemed to have forgotten that the island still hosted a murderer. In a way, all the guests had to some extent. The generation most of them were a part of had a real *but it won't happen to me* vibe. A conscious naivety – Richard thought that it wouldn't be a bad way to live, but he was too cynical for it. Too much damage already done. Brad, though, could be saved from the same feelings. He looked towards the lighthouse and then back towards the island's house, torn between the life he knew with Tara or the dream of a loving father and something new, maybe normal.

"Do you know who my dad is?" Brad said, stripping back the years even further and now appearing to Richard like a toddler. He had hoped the question wouldn't come. What did they say about white lies? They were okay if you had the right intentions. The information Richard had gathered wasn't his to tell, plus he wanted to make sure he was right about everything before opening his mouth. And even still, what would it do to Brad if he told him? The boy was facing an emotional crisis anyway, searching for a father he had built up in his head to be his saviour when he was the polar opposite. Now he faced finding out that the woman who raised him and meant more to him than anything in the world wasn't his mother. Richard hated having the power to keep the information to himself, but he knew it was the right thing to do.

"I know that your mum needs you Brad. Desperately." He held Brad's stare, jerking his head back towards the house to try and convince him. At the first and slight sign that he would move in that direction, Richard threw him the keys to the quad bike.

"Take this." He said, and Brad did.

Richard watched him go for a minute before turning back and striding towards the lighthouse. The anger and fear within him powered his legs to stride and it quickly came into view – the building stood tall and strong with no signs of giving in. He tried to keep composed, but the image of Ava's lifeless body kept flashing into his mind. He reached the lighthouse, the white stone walls looking dull in the moonlight, and pushed the heavy door inwards. At once, the atmosphere and its noise dropped. Richard felt the air get heavy, the pressure weighing on all of his senses. The door slotted shut behind him and he let his eyes adjust to the fresh darkness – no sign of anybody, yet. Scanning the room, he knew that he would have to make his way up the metal ladder. As he gripped one of the rungs, he heard familiar clicking footsteps above him. He had no choice but to climb up, exposing himself head-first to Ava's killer. Not just her killer, but the man who had sexually assaulted her as a vulnerable teenager, leaving her with a child that she begged a friend to raise.

Herbert had discovered Ava – in a sick way, it made sense that he was the one to take it all away.

36

Richard pulled himself up quickly, standing as far as possible from Herbert, who was still pacing. The lack of sleep and food paired with distress had allowed delirium to creep in, and he couldn't shake the image of the Scooby Doo cartoons he watched as a kid. Just like the murder mystery nights at his parent's house, Herbert had been hiding in plain sight. He publicly accused David of murder, trying to anger him and playing the victim. Word was that he burst into tears each time the detectives questioned him. Finally, he had played a part in De Rossi's story – giving quotes and offering a eulogy of sorts for Ava. He thought he could get away with it, and he almost had.

"I knew you were trouble. This all might've been avoided if it wasn't for you."

"Not like an abuser to pass the blame." Richard replied.

The moonlight was casting sharp shadows on Herb's face, making it hard to see where his eyes were focused. It would never occur to anybody to compare Brad's features with Herb's. Why would it? But with news of Ava having a child around the time Brad was born, her hatred for a man that had grown and grown since she was a teenager, and the picture of her beside Herbert on the day he discovered her talent, the whole story was finally as clear as the similarities between this man and the son he had forced on Ava. Richard had wondered what stopped Ava from sleeping some nights, and now the answer was staring him in the face.

"What were you going to do with Brad? Give him 17 years' worth of pocket money?"

"Depends on how much he knows." Herb answered.

"Why are you talking like this isn't all over? You think you're that bulletproof?"

"You get a thick skin over the years."

"Thick enough to murder your son's mother? To know that he's out there searching for you and do nothing about it? You do know Brad is yours, don't you?" Richard had to say it out loud to believe it himself.

"I had my suspicions."

"And Tara – does she know?"

"She's none the wiser. Thinks Ava was knocked up by some no-hoper boyfriend and didn't want it to ruin her career. Just think, that boyfriend could've been you. None of it – our little agreement - was a problem until this weekend." Herb said.

"She was going to out you?"

Herbert nodded and then shook his head in disappointment as if he'd found a fly in his soup or he had caught some local kids chapping his door and running away. A true monster – not one who stomped and roared, but one who refused to see the damage he'd done.

"She was starting a charity for battered women, and I was the springboard. A cruel thing to invite a man to his own funeral, don't you think? I couldn't stand for it."

"A charity?" Richard asked.

"You didn't know? It's the only reason you're here in the first place. You were to break the story."

She had read the piece about Jane and knew she could trust Richard to do it. He wasn't here to be helped, he was here to do the helping.

"She told you all of this?"

"Bits and pieces, and I gathered more from some others."

"And the drink spiking – that was you?"

"With a little help from my friends." Herb said, smiling because in his mind he was untouchable. De Rossi, maybe Bobby Taggart – but who else knew? Had Richard been battling against more people than he thought he was? "Hard enough to get time alone with her. All I had to do was make sure that yourself and that assistant had a good enough night to forget about her. You will forget about her, you know? This doesn't have to end any other way."

"You put Emily onto me? The Royal family line?"

Herb smiled wide, only now remembering the fun he had had in the run up to killing Ava.

"Making the best of a bad situation. Emily was another one of my discoveries – easily led, shall we say?"

"De Rossi." Richard said, spitting as he spoke as if the name left a bad taste. "What's he got to do with it all?"

"He scratches my back and you know how the rest goes."

"Meaning he knew you raped Ava and killed the story?"

"He knew we were together. How he interpreted it, I don't know."

"Does he know you killed her? He must've suspected it at least?"

"If he did, he didn't have the balls to do anything about it. Anyway, what could he do? He's been covering for me for years. That's how our little agreement works. I pass him stories, give him access to the stars. He sold his soul when he was a lad – and there's no going back."

"It wasn't just Ava, was it?" Richard knew the answer but wanted to hear it from the man himself. Herb didn't oblige, simply waving a big shovel-sized hand in response, sweeping the trauma of potentially hundreds of young women away like a bad smell.

Never before had his perception of someone changed this drastically – conversations with Herb days ago were like chatting to an uncle, now it felt like he was sharing a room with evil itself. The two of them seemed connected. When Herb moved left, Richard moved right – circling the room like it was a boxing ring. He had 20 years on the man, but probably gave away about 6 stone in weight. Herb also had nothing to lose. All things considered, he didn't fancy his chances if it came to a fight.

"Why kill her now after all these years? You must've known it was going to catch up with you one day."

"Are you a dog lover, Dick?" Herb asked, trying to hide the fact that he was edging ever so slightly closer to him. "I am. Always have been. We had a great pup called Rocky when I was growing up – my best friend, he was. We had a field close to the house that was all ridges – a hangover from the farming years before. Rocky would run over those ridges every day, and every day he came back with a limp. He didn't learn, did he? Eventually, his legs were buggered – no chance of repair. What were to do other than put him down?"

Richard refused to answer, even though he knew Herb didn't expect one.

"Ava was damaged – injured if you like. Just like Rocky, she wouldn't let go. Kept going back to the field of hurt. Her ending was written already, I just helped it along." Herb finished his point with a hint of pride.

"You're a sick bastard."

"See the problem with the righteous ones like yourself, you think everyone else holds themselves to the same standards. I've got news for you – us bastards don't think about that at all. And there are plenty more of us than there are you. That's why you'll never win."

Herb was no longer masking the fact that he was moving close to Richard. It made sense - the only real solution was getting rid of him as well. Maybe he would use it to his advantage – tell the police that Richard had admitted to the murder and they had got into an altercation. That could only happen if Richard lost, and he didn't plan to let that happen. For years he had stood shouting from the sidelines, making valiant efforts to stand up and be counted but never following through when it came to it. His sister had been snatched from him, his credibility next and now Ava – the woman whose memory he had romanticized so much over the last couple of days that he was convinced was the love of his life. Now, this was increasingly looking like his last chance to do something more than talking.

The talking was done, and both men knew it. As if there was

a silent pact, they moved towards each other – Richard visibly more uncomfortable than the killer he was squaring up to. Herb struck first, bringing his fist back and recoiling it at double the speed. He had aimed for Richard's eye and immediately opened the wound. Half blind, he swung back and caught the air, taking his weight with him. His shoulder connected with Herb's barrel chest and knocked him back slightly, but it gave him an opening for another pounding right hand to Richard's eye socket. This time, he felt something break. The pain shot through his body and jerked at his spine. Again, the movement helped to push Herb back, but only so far.

"She put up more of a fight than you, son."

Son. There was that word again. He closed his fist and brought it upwards, connecting with Herb's jaw. This time, he felt it and staggered backwards towards the rust covered brick.

"You don't like when I mention her do you?" Herb spat, rubbing his jaw as if he was snapping it back into place. "What if I told you how I did it?"

Richard didn't take the bait – instead he took the chance for a breath.

"I can't decide what was easier, you know – killing her or getting her into bed."

Herb had picked up a hefty stone now. He made it to Richard in three strides, confident enough that he had no energy left to keep up the fight. As he raised the rock behind his shoulder, Richard dug into his pocket, bypassing the active audio recorder and grabbing the pen. Herb brought the lump across with all his might. As it connected with Richard's broken face, he stabbed the pen deep into the recess between Herb's collarbone and neck. Dazed, Richard staggered back, just about keeping his balance until he fell into a sitting position. His eyes were spinning, but he caught sight of the pen sticking out of Herb's chest like an old light switch. He had given all he had, and he wasn't the one standing. He hoped for Herb to topple, but a swaying back and forth as he felt the damage with his fingertips was all that came.

Richard's eyelids drooped and everything went black. He

forced them back open and Herb was closer.

"You weren't built for this, son - " as the final word came out his mouth, he was tackled at the waist and sent tumbling. Chief Inspector Murphy was taking no chances. He pummeled Herb's head and body with thundering blows until breath was the only thing left in there. He muttered a line that he probably had cocked and loaded for the entirety of his police career. Richard wished he had heard it, but his head was back against the stone floor as he drifted into unconsciousness.

RECOVERY

37

He feared that there were some memories from the island that he would never get back, but the more he thought about it the more it seemed like a good thing.

One thing he wished he would forget was calling Chief Inspector Murphy 'Dad' as they were waiting for assistance. He'd decided to close that particular box and leave it for a Counsellor to deal with in ten years. Not that that would be the only thing to need unpacking. Richard had been less kind to DI Rankin. He had tossed the audio recorder with Herb's confession to him and muttered something sarcastic. Rankin informed him that it was gibberish and he likely had a concussion, but Richard thought it was just because he didn't have a comeback. His general demeanor could've been described as lucid and airy, which had shocked some people considering what he had just been through. The paramedic in the helicopter had explained that it was just one of the many ways some people dealt with shock – he then warned him that there would be a big downward spiral to come. It wasn't a very comforting thing to hear in a helicopter. Herb was alive and Richard had decided he was glad about that as long as he faced appropriate punishment. Of that, he wasn't sure – his eyes had been open to the flaws of law and order, hierarchies and power dynamics. It wasn't pretty. Neither was he – he had fractured his orbital bone and now boasted a titanium implant on his eye socket. The Doctor had informed him that the punches wouldn't have done it on their own, but the area was fragile from the beer can hitting it. That train journey had seemed like years ago, never mind days. Still, it felt fitting to him that an injury from his life before the island contributed to his state now – the showdown with Herb was, after all, a culmination of many things for Richard. Ava had just been the spark.

He had kept his phone off after a quick call to his Dad – his real one, not a confused and slightly embarrassed police chief. The truth was that he wasn't ready to deal with whatever had to come next. The police, the media, the public. He wasn't sure he ever would be. Since he was a boy, Richard had looked to test himself – to prove that he would choose fight over flight. He had finally done that, and the reality was that he didn't know if he ever could again. Knowing the consequences and what it took made it even scarier than what the main reluctance was before - the mystery.

The police were confident that Herb would be going to prison. His chaperoning officer had also let slip that De Rossi would likely be charged with accessory to murder. He would plead ignorance, but Richard didn't buy it and wasn't sure a jury would either. Still, he was a smooth talker and had survived this far. He knew one thing – he'd be out and writing for the tabloids again in no time if his case falls on DI Rankin's desk. Richard's only hope was that Herb would bring De Rossi down with him like the sidekick he was. Not only had he gotten to the point of needing Herb to survive, he did whatever asked of him. That included the spiking of the drinks and encouragement of the bizarre royal family lie, the one which Richard felt sick when he thought of how it had made him laugh. He had been convinced it was the two of them that had met in the castle that night until Murphy described somebody more like Bobby Taggart being seen with Herb. Another enemy for Richard to carry forward. At least people now knew he wasn't a killer, although the paper – as they always did – had stayed just on the fringes of accusation enough that they would never need to print an apology or a retraction.

The drugs were starting to kick in again. Mary and Ava were in the room with him now, perched on either side of the bed at his feet. They looked over him with worry. Mary looked as she always had – a picture of perfection created solely by his imagination based on scant memories. He wanted to speak to her, to ask her if she had saw what happened. *I didn't cry this time.* He would say. *I didn't just stand there.* Still, it had all been too late – as the figure beside her reminded him. Beautiful Ava, wearing the outfit and with the swagger that she had walked onto the balcony with at the party. Richard knew now that she would've been nervous about what was to come. He had played out the alternate reality in his head a few times now – her announcement going to plan. He had doubted she would've named Herb in front of the crowd but would've alluded to it in such a way that most people would know what he had put her through. Richard had learnt since that the charity she was starting was called RE-EMPOWER and would focus on helping young women in the entertainment business. His experience over the weekend told him that it was necessary. He had seen a lot of rivalry and toxicity on the island, and it was born out of a need to be the best, because there just weren't enough seats at the table. On top of that, what some of them had to go through to get those seats wasn't worth a lifetime of fame and riches. He had briefly considered getting involved in the project and starting from where she left off, but he could already hear the cries of *white male saviour* and had to agree with them. There were more fitting people, and far more capable, that could carry the torch from here. Maybe Hayley or Tara. The only plan Richard wanted to make when he got out of the hospital was to meet her. She had broken her leg in three places, but it seemed she would walk again. Some of the bruising and cuts sounded worse. Still, if Herb had his way she would be gone for good and Brad would have nothing or nobody at all. Herb – the nice father figure. Uncle Herbert. Someone all the young women in the industry could trust. An open secret, some of the papers had called it. It put Richard on the edge of vomiting. The idea that there were people on that island, or off it, that could have pointed the finger at Herb and didn't was the sign of a losing battle against evil.

His head was heavy now – too heavy for his weary neck to keep it up. His eye twinged with pain. They said that would happen. He closed it to try and temper the suffering, and the other followed. He didn't bother trying to open them again.

38

Richard took a seat outside the café on this visit, knowing it would be easier for Tara to navigate in her wheelchair, which she had mentioned would be temporary on the phone. He sipped the coffee and smiled at an old couple walking by. As they moved past, they bickered about replacing a set of curtains. He wondered if he would ever allow himself to be occupied by the small things. Was he doomed to carry the world's anxiety on his shoulders for the rest of his years? As his eye recovered in the hospital, they treated him for dehydration as well. Regardless of the island, his body wasn't in a good way. Now, although still tender, he felt a bit fitter. The promise he made himself to get in good shape still hung in the back of his mind. Coming out of a fight second best with a man twenty-five years older will do that to you. The requests for comment had slowed now, but would come back around when Herb was put on trial. He had sent a text to De Rossi, knowing he wouldn't see it for a while. It simply read *Looking for a quote – would love to tell your story.* Petty and childish? Yes, but satisfying too. It was likely he would never know how deep his involvement went. The fact that he didn't dig was his worst crime. His other text, to Tara, had been responded to quickly. She seemed as eager as he was to meet, although probably for a different reason entirely. When she had phoned to arrange, there was no indication whether or not she was living in Glasgow with Brad, and he had a feeling that she wouldn't be offering information on their permanent residence to anyone in a hurry.

A taxi pulled up right outside the café, holding up the traffic on the narrow West End street. The driver slid the door and attached the ramp, allowing Tara to roll down carefully. Behind her, Brad ducked his head out of the car and waited for her to reach the pavement before offering to push her. Tara shooed him off and pointed at Richard. Brad approached, one hand grabbing the other and eyes looking at everything except the man in front of him. He had been told to thank him. Richard remembered detesting such orders when he was Brad's age, so simply extended his hand. Brad shook it and gave a short nod. No point in putting the boy through any more embarrassment. He went inside and sat at a free table, ordering a fizzy drink when asked. Another manoeuvre they had clearly discussed in the cab. Richard stood and moved the spare chair away as Tara tipped the driver and waved an apology at the building queue of cars. On seeing they had been beeping at someone in a wheelchair, a few held up their hands and bowed their heads.

"I could get used to this." Tara said as she slotted herself into the space he'd made.

"Are you going to have to?"

"For a while, then plenty of rehab. How are you?"

"Part man, part robot. A bit like the Terminator, really."

"Brad loves that – I'll need to tell him."

Richard knew that she babied him, and that he probably hadn't watched the films for years. Still, better to have someone care for you like that than to have nobody care for you at all.

"What can I get you?" Richard waved his phone with the café's ordering app.

"Cappuccino, thanks. God, it'll get to a point where we don't need to talk to anyone for anything."

Richard smiled, but imagined her finishing that sentence by saying that it would be ideal. Who could blame her for wanting to protect herself and her son from the world? He ordered the drinks, getting himself his third black coffee of the day to combat the slow-motion effect his painkillers were having.

"I owe you an explanation." Tara said. Richard agreed to an extent, so he stayed quiet to let it come.

212

"Maybe now we can sit here and say that if I had told the police that Brad was Ava's son it would've all been over quicker, but I made a promise to her. Plus, I couldn't work out in my head how it connected to her death at all."

"You didn't know about Herb being the father?"

"No. Which means she didn't tell anybody – she just swallowed it and moved on."

"So what did she say?"

"Ava was a star even before she was a star – everybody knew it. I remember her first day on set, there was a kind of stunned silence after we wrapped. The crew had never seen a presence like hers. I'd left school early and had been a runner on these shows for a year or so. They asked me to hang around with her backstage, so that she had someone her own age." The coffees arrived and Tara took an immediate sip, wincing slightly at the heat. Richard let his cool.

"Now that I think about it, it might even have been him who asked me to show her around."

"Herb?"

"Yeah. Like everyone else, I thought he was one of the good ones. Anyway, we grew close. I'd left most of my friends behind at school and was desperate for someone who was working to spend my time with. I always felt a bit older than my years. We rented a flat together – it was like a film."

Richard took a sip of his coffee, ashamed at everything he had missed from Ava's life just because she had left him to pursue a dream.

"One night she came home in tears – she told me that she was pregnant and she didn't know what to do. She wouldn't even give abortion a second thought, but she worried for her career. How sad is that? That she thought she couldn't have both? And she was right." Richard nodded in agreement.

"So who did you think was the father?"

"Honestly?" She looked down, almost embarrassed. "I thought it was you."

Richard wasn't as shocked as she thought he would be. In

fact, he knew that was pretty much the consensus among Ava's nearest and dearest.

"Brad said that when you were drunk - or drugged, rather – that you told him his father was on the island."

"God, I know. He's still asking me about it. I'm denying the memory."

"But it was me you were talking about, not Herb." Richard nodded as he spoke, still putting the pieces together. "Weren't you weary of me being there given what you thought you knew?"

"I trusted Ava with everything I have. She told me not to worry, so I didn't."

"And at no point you thought I'd killed her?"

"No – which led me to believe that the whole thing had nothing to with the secret about Brad."

"You didn't think she was lying at the time? When she first told you?"

"I didn't push it. She said it was complicated and an old boyfriend. Hand on my heart, I didn't think for a second that she had been raped." Both of them had danced around saying the word up until that point. It hung in the air like a poison cloud.

"If she had I would've taken her straight to the police. Remember, I felt like it was my job to protect her."

"You were eighteen as well – whole life ahead of you... What made you take on the responsibility of raising the baby?" It had been something that Richard couldn't figure out.

"I loved her, Richard. Not in a way I was used to, or that was expected, but I loved Ava in a way that I would do anything to help her, and to keep her around."

Richard had felt the same in his teenage years. He had no doubt that if they hadn't gone their separate ways that he would've fallen into that same love.

"It didn't start out like that anyway. We raised him together, I was just the mum in public. I started using contacts because he had eyes as blue as hers. I went everywhere with Ava, so it meant that Brad could as well. That's how it started – the three of us

214

against everyone. In the beginning I think she resented him because of what Herbert did, but it wasn't long until she absolutely adored him, and so did I. But the whole point of the arrangement was that she could keep working, so after a year or so she went back. It changed from there – the ratio of work and motherhood. Eventually we decided that when he was old enough, he'd call me mum. Why put the burden of the secret on his shoulders? We were in too deep, honestly."

Richard thought back to first meeting Tara – judging her as an organised bore, so in control that nothing exciting or spontaneous could ever happen. How he had been proven wrong.

"That hurt Ava, of course. It caused a lot of fights over the years. Sometimes she would decide that she wanted to pack it all in and come clean to Brad. I think she was getting closer to that idea than ever."

"And how did you feel about it?"

"Sad. Confused. I'm not sure. I can't help but think about what I've missed out on. If I could talk to eighteen-year-old me right now, what advice would I give her? Don't do it? I don't know."

Richard couldn't offer any advice, and knew that it would be wrong to try. They sat in silence for a minute or two, the sun coming out of the clouds. Tara smiled at a mother pushing a pram and the woman smiled back.

"And Ava's parents – how much do they know?"

At that, Tara bit her lip slightly signalling a real sort point.

"They think the baby was adopted and that was that. They were hurt. I think they still are. But if you're asking if they know Brad's their grandson? No." She admitted.

For the first time in recent memory, Richard was glad he had his own problems to deal with. They were nowhere near as complicated as this.

"How is he?" Richard said, nodding towards the window. Tara had only taken her eyes off Brad's table for seconds at a time.

"He's having some trust issues. He knows there's something I'm not telling him."

"Have you decided how much you're going to tell?"

"You can't imagine the situation I'm in."

"I know – I'd never judge you either way."

"On one hand I want him to know that his Mum was a great woman – someone who wanted to change the world for the better. On the other, that would mean admitting that I'd been lying to him his whole life. It would mean that he would look at me differently, maybe even leave me."

Tara's eyes looked like those of a woman ten years older, and Richard knew that she was scared. The woman had spent years helping everyone around her, putting out their fires, but when she was finally faced with her own she didn't know what to do.

"And his father?" He asked.

"He's going to keep asking – what would you do?"

"I'm not sure. The boy's been through a hell of a lot, most of which he doesn't even really know about. He loves you though – I knew that when he had the chance to find out about his dad, but ran to you because you were hurt. That should tell you all you need to know. He's a good kid."

"Do you believe that sort of thing can be – passed down? What Herbert did – could it be inside Brad somewhere?"

"I think the environment creates the monster, nothing else. Now Brad has the best anyone could ask for. In fact, he always has." Richard nodded at Tara as he said it. Her smile reminded him of Ava's. Just modest enough, but still accepting.

"What are you going to do?" She asked him. She checked on Brad again, who was engrossed with the screen of his phone.

"I've got a few things that I need to work on." It wasn't clear whether he meant personally or through work, and that's because he meant both.

"And Ava's story?"

Richard didn't respond. He had thought this over in his head and been back and forth between answers. Today it was that no, he wouldn't tell Ava's story. In fact, it had been a part of the reason he wanted to meet Tara.

"She wanted you to, you know." Tara continued.

"These things have a tendency to be sensationalised – I wouldn't want to do that to her. Reduce her to a headline."

"So do it your way."

"I'd never mention Brad, if you're worried about that."

"I knew you wouldn't."

There was an something going unmentioned that made Richard uncomfortable. Ava's secret had died with her, but Herb was still alive and he was about to become the most scrutinised man in the country, not to mention the fact that the police now knew about the pregnancy. She had made it clear that she didn't want to tell Brad, but it was inevitable he would find out very soon. He thought about letting it go, but didn't know if he would ever see her again. Maybe she had been so emotional that the reality hadn't hit her. It was better coming from him.

"Are you worried about the trial? That you'll have to testify?"

She nodded very slightly, a tear forming in the corner of each eye. Of course she had thought about it. Of course she knew that there was a fresh hell still to come. She may not be accepting of it, but soon she'd have no choice. He wondered how the contact lenses felt, how she felt taking them out at night when Brad had gone to bed and putting them in all over again before he woke up.

"I'm terrified."

Richard, still thinking about the contact lenses, couldn't think of one thing to say to console her.

"How can he still be ruining lives?" She asked. He knew he had to speak, to offer something.

"What he's done won't stop when he's in prison. There are lifetimes of hurt to be felt even after he's gone. I wish I could tell you it would all be okay, or that Brad won't find out. Really though? He will. And it'll scare you both. All you can do is offer the love he deserves and give him time. What's going to happen then I don't know, but it's all you can do."

"I wasn't sure about you – why she insisted on having you there. I get it now." Tara said.

"Do you? I'm not sure I do."

"You're not afraid to see the bad side of things. In fact, it's like you almost expect it."

"And that's a good thing?" Richard asked.

"In a world full of people who make themselves believe there's no bad, yeah I'd say we need you."

Richard smiled.

"No fun at parties to be fair, but everyone has their purpose." She added.

He smiled wider, so Tara joined him. It was nice for them to take a brief holiday from the drama, however short lived it would be. She finished her drink and tapped the window with a dainty finger. Brad shot up and made for the door. Richard had stopped hoping for the best for himself a long time ago, but the hope was still there. He found himself finding others to wish it upon, and for now he would pile it on to Tara and young Brad. He reached the table and shot an arm out to shake Richard's hand again. It made Richard smile. He took it and gave a firm squeeze.

"Take care of your mum." He said. Brad puffed his chest a bit and nodded. He would be okay.

"Are you hanging around?" Tara said, as she wheeled herself away from the table and used all of her wrist strength to manage the uneven city pavements.

"I'm waiting for someone." Richard said. He waved the two of them off and watched as they headed towards the park. Blood or no blood, he had never seen a better picture of a mother and son together.

Alone again, he sipped his coffee already thinking about the next. He didn't hold out much hope for this meeting. He watched the people pass, all with their own problems and brave faces. Too much to take on, he told himself – worry about you. He knew he wouldn't. *Solve other people's problems and lock yours away,* the more authoritative voice in his head said. He heard a pair of heels approaching from behind him and shut his eyes as the sound became louder. Was it that he didn't think she would turn up, or that deep down he didn't want her to? The time to answer was gone as Jane grabbed a seat and sat down across from him. Fight it was, he thought. He had never liked flying anyway.

A NOTE FROM THE AUTHOR

I started this story knowing one thing - a superstar was to be killed at their birthday party. Whilst filling the blanks it became clear that I was addressing some big issues, and my genuine hope is that I did so with compassion and care. If you come away feeling introspective and the book provokes thoughts and conversations, it's a success in my mind. Despite its dark nature, I had fun writing it and hope you did reading it. Currently, I'm continuing the story of Richard 'Dick' Dickson because I think there's more to tell. If you agree, please leave a review of the book. A simple thing that helps a great deal. You can buy the second book in the series - Eyes in the Shadows - now.

This was a debut that came about from the death of my mother, who always wanted to write. I took that dream on. If you find it raw or unconventional, that's because it is. I hope you'll come on the journey with me.

Thanks for reading.

AF Kerr

BOOKS IN THIS SERIES

Richard Dickson Investigations

Death Of An Influencer

A superstar's party on a private island takes a sinister turn when a body is found battered and bruised on the beach, and the police arrive to lockdown the guests until they find the killer. Surrounded by people who would like to see his downfall, Richard Dickson must put the pieces together before the police arrest him or, worse still, he becomes the second victim.

Eyes In The Shadows

Journalist Richard Dickson's mental state is spiralling downwards. His desire to get out of his head and into a story leads him to Dr Charles Mee – a respected therapist with a wretched private life. The therapist, thrown out of his marital home, enlists Richard's help to identify a stalker whose threats are becoming more sinister by the day. When the stalker begins to close in, Richard Dickson can save a life – he just isn't sure there are any worth saving.

Printed in Great Britain
by Amazon

79817771R00139